THE MARRIAGE BARGAIN

When Elinor is forced to marry William de Valences, it is for her lands, not her beauty. But King Henry makes it a condition of marriage that William should provide proof of Guy de Riddington's plotting with the French. William falls in love with his wife, but suspects that squire Robert Latimer is her lover. William rids himself of his rival and keeps his bargain with the king, leaving him and Elinor free to enjoy married life together.

LISA ANDREWS

THE MARRIAGE BARGAIN

Complete and Unabridged

LINFORD
Leicester

First published in Great Britain in 2005

First Linford Edition
published 2006

British Library CIP Data

Andrews, Lisa
   The marriage bargain.—Large print ed.—
Linford romance library
   1. Forced marriage—Fiction
   2. Love stories
   3. Large type books
   I. Title
   823.9′14 [F]

   ISBN 1–84617–375–2

Published by
F. A. Thorpe (Publishing)
Anstey, Leicestershire

Set by Words & Graphics Ltd.
Anstey, Leicestershire
Printed and bound in Great Britain by
T. J. International Ltd., Padstow, Cornwall

This book is printed on acid-free paper

1

As soon as the crowd of women left the chamber, Elinor wrenched her night-gown back over her head.

'If you're cold, you should climb into bed, my lady,' her nurse remonstrated, but Elinor ignored her.

It was late summer and even the thick stones of the castle radiated warmth.

'There's no air in here. It's like a prison.'

She flung back the shutter that covered the arrow slit and breathed in the balmy stillness. Meg clucked disapprovingly.

'If I'd been free to do so, I never would have married him.'

She let the shutter slip back as the smell of the moat filtered upwards.

'Lord preserve us! Don't speak such things.'

'Why not? You told me I should always speak the truth.'

Meg decided to change the subject.

'You've such pretty hair, as rich and shining as the chestnuts on the tree.'

Elinor gave a short laugh.

'Oh, yes, my hair. Even my new husband managed to compliment me on that. Why was that, do you think?'

'Because it's true. Everyone tells you so.'

'Oh, yes, everyone tells me how pretty my hair is because they can't say the same about my face.'

Meg sighed.

'You're overwrought, child, else you wouldn't say such things. You looked lovely today. If only your dear mother was here to see it.'

'Don't speak of my mother.'

A sudden chill entered the chamber and Elinor shivered.

'You should get into bed.'

Meg brushed rose petals from the coverlet.

'It isn't time.'

'It'll be warmer.'

'I'm not cold.'

Meg sat heavily on the side of the bed.

'Child, you're stubborn. Promise me you won't act so with your husband.'

'Do you think it matters to him how I act?'

Meg gave her a look.

'I'm certain it does.'

Elinor shrugged.

'Why on earth have you taken against him so?' Meg insisted. 'Any woman in this castle would exchange places with you. Is he not handsome?'

'Is he not arrogant?'

Meg couldn't deny it.

'Is he not a fine warrior?' she tried instead.

'He has the reputation of allowing nothing to stand in his way, I believe.'

Meg closed her eyes momentarily.

'And does he not hold the king's favour?'

'Yes, he does, and how fortunate for him, for without it he would be nothing.'

Meg rushed to the curtain that hung at the door of the chamber and swept it back. Satisfied that no-one was listening, she replaced it and walked back into the room.

'I beseech you to mind your tongue, my lady. What do you mean, he's nothing? He's the son of a lord.'

'He's the youngest son, and his father's lands had already been divided before he was born. Without the king's favour he'd be just another hearth knight dependent on another for the food he ate.'

Meg sat on a stool and folded her arms.

'Why are you so upset?'

'You can ask that when today my lands were handed to another, and I was handed to a stranger who has the right to do with me whatever he wishes?'

Meg looked unimpressed.

'Since your brother's and then your father's death, you knew how this would be. You knew that this morning

4

and you weren't so upset then. What's happened?'

Elinor hesitated, but decided it was unfair to burden the older woman.

'Nothing.'

'You forget, child, I've known you these past twenty years.'

She sighed.

'My new husband, Lord William de Valences, great warrior and favourite of the king, thinks I'm stupid.'

'Nay, my lady, I'm certain that's not right.'

'He thinks I'm stupid and he laughed at me.'

Meg pursed her lips as Elinor continued.

'He laughed when I told him I couldn't read or write, and now he thinks I'm stupid as well as plain. Without my lands he'd never have looked twice at me.'

'Now you can't know that's so.'

'Really? Then where is my fine husband now?'

'I'm sure there's a reason he's not

here. He's probably with the king. A man can't just up and leave when the king's at his table, you know.'

Elinor kept silent and, mistaking her silence for assent, Meg warmed to her theme.

'Like as not, they've matters of state to discuss. What an important man your husband is that King Henry can't do without him even at this hour.'

Elinor sighed. The loftiest matter her husband was likely to be discussing with the king was the quality of the wine they were drinking. Silently she hoped that it would choke him.

'And what an honour it was that the king himself chose your husband and graced your marriage table. There isn't — '

Elinor could stand it no longer.

'Aye, he graced my marriage table and spent most of the feast eyeing me as if I were a piece of meat on it.'

'Holy Mother, your tongue'll be the death of us both!'

Meg swept a nervous glance at the chamber door.

'It's true. He looked at me more than William did. I know I'm no beauty, but for just one day he could have pretended he wanted more than my lands.'

Meg rose from the stool and wrapped her arms around her.

'You're as lovely as a spring morn, child. Any man who can't see it is a fool.'

Elinor was soothed but not fooled by her nurse's words. She'd been teased often enough by her brother and his friends about her plainness.

'I do love you, Meg.'

She held on to the surprised woman a moment longer. This would be the first night ever that her nurse wouldn't sleep in the truckle bed at her feet. She would not miss her snoring but she'd miss her comforting presence in the room.

'And I you, child. Now, will you get into bed?'

Elinor raised her arms and allowed Meg to strip off the nightgown, then climbed into bed.

'Now just a little drop of this. I think I hear your husband coming.'

'What is it?' She sniffed suspiciously at the vial.

'Poppy juice and valerian. It'll help you to do your duty.'

Elinor shook her head. Her fears had already made her drink more wine than she should at the marriage feast. She dared drink nothing more.

'In case you change your mind.' Meg placed it beside the bed.

'Go now, Meg.'

'Yes, my lady.' Meg kissed her and went.

Finally, Elinor was alone with her thoughts. They'd been there all day but she'd been too busy to give them heed. Now they claimed her full attention and it was all she could do to resist jumping out of bed and calling Meg back. She clasped her hands in prayer, then unclasped them moments later. Had her own mother prayed like this on her wedding night? And would her own fate be the same as hers? Unconsciously, she twisted the sheet between her fingers then stared, horrified, at the rose petals that smeared a blood-red stain over the white linen. Shuddering, she wondered whether nine months from now her wedding sheets would serve as her shroud. Would she die in childbirth as her mother had done before her?

The sound of laughter penetrated her panic. Male laughter — her husband was finally making his way to bed. She was terrified out of her wits. Once again, she closed her eyes and mumbled a prayer.

The laughter grew louder and more raucous. Just how many attendants did he bring with him? Would they stare at her and imagine themselves in his place? Or would they not want to? Was that why they were laughing?

The men gathered outside her chamber door. It was the same instant that her gaze fell on the vial of poppy juice and valerian, and between then and the moment they entered, she gripped the vial and emptied the contents down her throat.

'Greetings, Lady de Valences.'

Elinor pulled the sheets to her chin and stared at King Henry. If she'd known that he intended to come to her chamber, she'd never have let Meg remove her nightgown. She glanced at it now as it lay folded on a stool and saw Henry follow her gaze, his mouth curved in amusement.

'Good evening, sire,' she managed, and flushed a deep scarlet.

If the king expected her to rise from the bed and drop him a curtsey then he was sorely mistaken. Her husband had the right to see her naked but the rest of these men, and that included the highest in the land, did not. Henry turned to her husband.

'By God, William, I envy you tonight.'

Her husband made no answer, but his eyes caught hers and a curious half-smile played on his lips. Elinor flushed harder but this time with anger.

Did he laugh at her still? She studied the savagely handsome face but couldn't tell.

The king himself took off William's over-tunic of richly-embroidered blue silk and the Earl of Gloucester kneeled on the pelt-covered floor to unbuckle his sword belt.

'My noble lords, please do not trouble yourselves. It's some years since I mastered the art of undressing.'

But his laughing protest went unheeded. A moment more and William de Valences stood before them as naked as a new-born. She kept her eyes levelled on his face. His steady blue gaze seemed to command it. Naked, he lost none of the imperiousness that struck everyone that met him.

The king thumped him on the back.

'We'll leave you to your pleasures and seek our own. Good-night and good sport!'

When the door thudded behind them, William ran his fingers through his dark hair and gave her a smile that might have been self-deprecating in one less proud.

'How is it with you, Elinor?' he enquired softly.

She fought the weariness in her limbs and tried to return the smile.

'Well, my lord.'

'William,' he corrected, and then, 'Do you forgive me?'

Her gaze fluttered up to his. Why should he ask forgiveness from her?

'I don't know that there's anything yet to forgive,' she answered carefully, and was rewarded by another smile.

'I'm pleased to hear it. I thought perhaps that leaving a bride so long alone on her wedding night might give cause for complaint. It was intended as no insult, I assure you.'

Elinor wanted to ask his reason for doing so, but seemed incapable of forming the words. When she didn't answer, his gaze swept about the room, freeing her own to study him. She took in the broad shoulders and tightly-packed musculature of his chest before halting at an angry scar that ran the length of his left arm. Whoever had stitched it had been no master of the art. He picked up a goblet of wine, took a drink, and offered it to her. She shook her head.

He put it down before sitting on the bed and, with gentle pressure, prised the sheets from her grasp.

'Are you afraid of me, Elinor?' he murmured.

Again she shook her head.

'Good.'

He bent to brush his lips against hers. The touch of him was like the tickling of a feather, but the scent of him was warm, musky and dangerous. Deep within her something unknown, something mysterious stirred. If only she wasn't so tired. If only she could keep her eyes from closing.

'I'm happy to do my duty, my lord,' she sighed.

She felt his mouth widen and heard the vibration of his suppressed laughter.

'That gladdens me, my lady, for I am

more than happy to do my own,' and with that, he climbed into bed beside her.

*   *   *

Was she ill? She woke to find every stonemason in the land chipping pieces from her skull. She'd never experienced anything so painful. With a sob, she called Meg's name.

'Your servant isn't here.'

The deep, masculine voice cut into her senses.

She sat up in bed, realised that she wasn't wearing her nightgown, and slid beneath the sheets again. Slowly, for the pain in her head made it impossible to do it otherwise, she turned and saw her husband sitting by the window.

'Good morning, wife.'

She stared at him as he came towards her. His voice was mild but the expression in his eyes was thunderous.

'I think I'm ill.'

'Aye, and by your own hand.'

14

With a jerk, he snatched the vial from the coffer by the bed.

'Tell me what this contained.'

'Poppy juice and valerian.'

'Poppy juice and valerian,' he repeated with total disdain. 'Seeing their effect last night, it surprises me you ever woke up this morning.'

Elinor stifled a groan. Feeling their effect on her body, it might have been better if she hadn't.

'Who mixed this potion? Who was responsible for this foul brew?'

He grabbed her wrist. She gulped nervously but wouldn't betray Meg.

'I mixed it.'

'Was the thought of me in your bed so repulsive that you'd rather chance oblivion?'

'No.'

He let go her wrist but his sapphire-hard eyes still held hers.

'Then explain, if you please.'

She gazed up at him through a fan of half-lowered lashes.

'I'm truly sorry, William.'

Abruptly he turned away, and she tensed, waiting for what he would do next. Her brother would have rained blows on her. Gilbert couldn't bear to be thwarted in any matter and she'd thought this man the same.

'I'm sorry,' she repeated.

His back was towards her but she fancied that the muscles across his shoulders eased slightly.

'So am I.'

He walked back to the window. She pulled the coverlet up to her chin and felt her face flush a deeper red. His face, too, had flushed a deep crimson, but the cause was anger rather than embarrassment.

She couldn't meet his gaze and stared instead at her white taut knuckles gripping the coverlet.

'Look at me, Elinor!' he said when her eyes remained resolutely cast downwards. 'I know your fear. Do I look the kind of man who would bed an insensible woman?'

The answer he undoubtedly wanted

was no, but she summoned her courage.

'I don't know, William. I know nothing at all about you.'

Anger flashed through his eyes and then abruptly died.

'You're right, of course. Perhaps I was expecting too much.'

He released her, and she wondered exactly what it was he'd expected. Whatever it was, she'd disappointed him. It came as a surprise to realise how much she wished she hadn't.

'Know one thing, lady,' he continued, 'if I had bedded you, you wouldn't have any doubt as to what took place.'

The laughter that accompanied this statement was mocking, but she wasn't sure to whom it was directed. He swept an elaborate bow.

'Now that I'm assured you aren't in any danger from the potion you drank last night, I'll take my leave of you.'

'You can't!'

'Indeed I must. Your desire to keep

me in your chamber is touching, but I needs must go.'

'But the marriage hasn't been consummated!'

'No.'

'It has to be!'

His expression darkened.

'Indeed, it will, but not this morning.'

He began to walk towards the door and, in a panic lest he should leave, she leaped out of bed and ran after him. He caught her in his arms and pressed her tightly against his chest before drawing her to arms' length to view her body.

'You are very beautiful, wife. How I wish I weren't already too late.'

She crossed her arms over her body and was certain that the pink flooding her cheeks had continued down to her toes.

He caught her in his arms and pulled her to him, and at that moment she felt a spark kindle in the depths of her being. She felt her heart stir, like a dying ember fanned into flame by a breath of wind. She lifted her face to look into his and guessed his intent. He would kiss her and, to her surprise, she rose to the tips of her toes to assist him.

The kiss was honey sweet, but, oh, too short. His lips pressed but once against hers before they pulled away again.

'I do believe that we might deal well together,' he murmured. 'I regret that I must leave you at this time.'

'Then stay.'

The act between them had to be done, would be done, so why not now? Her body tingled strangely at his touch and last night's terror had died away.

'Truly, I can't.'

He gripped her shoulders and rested his brow on hers.

'King Henry orders my absence and I must obey. I swear to you that it isn't how I'd choose to begin my wedded life.'

'Nor I.'

The unfamiliar masculine scent of him tantalised her senses. He was different to any other man she'd ever encountered, taller, more warrior-like, more certain of his own worth, and yet, there was a softer side to his nature which she guessed not many had seen, and wouldn't see unless he chose to display it.

'How long?'

His expression became veiled.

'A week, perhaps two. I hope it won't be more.'

All the emotion she'd kept tightly reined flooded through her — grief at her father's death, rage at being ordered to marry a man she'd never met, fear of what that might mean, and now disappointment that he was being taken from her before she could find out. She clenched her fists and turned her back on him so that he wouldn't see the tears in her eyes.

'I bid you farewell, my lord. I will endeavour to uphold your interests here while you're gone.'

For a long time there was silence, but she knew he was there. She was as aware of him as if she were facing him.

She could feel the strength of his will urging her to turn about and say farewell to him properly. She wouldn't. She wanted him to stay, and her soul raged at the power of men for controlling not only the affairs of her lands but also the affairs of her heart.

The anger in his voice was thinly masked when he spoke again.

'I'll take my leave of you, lady, and hope to find you in better temper on my return,' and, with a swish of the curtain that hung at the door of her chamber, he was gone.

2

Elinor accepted the squire's hand to help her into the saddle and swung agilely onto Fleur's back.

'Was it a messenger from court who arrived this morning?' he asked.

'No.' A glance at his face told her she hadn't answered the question to his satisfaction. Robert Latimer was persistent.

'So, no news yet of your husband?'

'No.'

'Eight weeks is a long time.'

'Nearer nine.'

If she hadn't known him better then she'd have sworn he was trying to upset her. But that was ridiculous. They'd played together as children. He'd been more like a brother to her than Gilbert ever had.

'Don't you think it's strange that he's never sent word that he's well or to enquire after you? For all he knows, you could even now be carrying his child.'

'You go too far, Robert!'

'Deepest apologies, Lady Elinor. The concern I have for you makes me over-bold. You know I wouldn't offend you for all the gold in Christendom. I love you like a sister.'

Elinor glanced at him sharply but only encountered a penitent smile. If rumours were to be believed then this man was her half-brother. Her father had never acknowledged him, but someone with wealth and influence must have paid the monks at Milchester Abbey for his keep. After Gilbert's death, he'd returned to the castle declaring that the life of a monk was not to his liking and that he was resolved to be a knight. But if her father, losing one son, had plans to substitute another then those plans had died with him. The sweating sickness had struck him shortly after Robert's return, and Robert's future now rested with the new lord of Elleston.

Looked at in this light, she realised

that he didn't mean to provoke her by his constant questions. Of course he'd be anxious for news of her husband. Nothing could be decided until his return.

'Forgive me?' Robert turned in his saddle to face her.

'Of course I forgive you, Robert.'

She frowned as the men-at-arms assembled in the bailey and she bent to stroke Fleur's nose in order to hide it. This was a game played out every morning. William had entrusted her safety to his own soldiers, who resented playing nursemaid to a woman and demonstrated it by arriving as late as they dared for escort duty. It was a minor matter, but one that her husband would be made aware of on his return.

'I hope we haven't kept you waiting, my lady.'

The captain swept her a smile that was as sly as it was insincere.

'Not at all. I prefer to take my time before riding out. I find it calms me.'

Elinor's smile matched the man's

own. He acknowledged it with a brief nod before laying his hand on her bridle.

'I would ask you to limit your riding to the estate, Lady Elinor.'

Elinor jerked the bridle out of his grasp. Why did he make a point of reminding her every single day? Granted, she could be headstrong at times, but she wasn't entirely witless. Guy de Riddington, whose estates bordered hers, or rather her husband's now, was a cruel tyrant of a man. She had no desire to be captured riding on his lands and rendered hostage to him.

'Don't you think that your men are equal to the task of protecting me?'

'No harm will come to you, my lady, providing that you stay on our land.'

Elinor resisted a shudder. How was it that the man's assurance always sounded like threats?

'His advice is sound. These are troubled times, my lady,' a voice murmured at her shoulder.

She stared at its owner. She didn't think Robert Latimer cared any more for the man than she did.

'I don't wish to alarm you, Lady Elinor, but would it not be wise to send a messenger for news of your husband?' Robert continued.

'Why?'

Robert cleared his throat.

'Perhaps he's been so long absent because he's dead.'

Dead? William de Valences? As she lived and breathed, she knew with a certainty that her husband did the same.

'I think I'd have been informed if my lord had died,' she answered coldly.

But why didn't he return? She only had to remember their wedding night and her leave-taking of him to gain a clue, but no matter how difficult the situation became in the castle, the sun would drop from the sky before she sent word and begged him to come back.

As soon as they clattered across the drawbridge and Elinor sniffed the salt tang of the sea, she urged Fleur into a gallop. Winter was tightening its grip on the land and riding out might soon be impossible but she'd continue as long as she could. The palfrey had been a wedding gift from William, sure-footed as befitted a lady's mount, but with an added spark and liveliness that was pure joy. Elinor adored her. Whatever else her errant husband might be, he was an excellent judge of horseflesh.

Her cheeks were glowing and her wimple askew when they arrived at the first village. She took a moment to arrange herself before accepting Robert's hand to dismount. Already two little girls were running towards her and screeching with joy at her arrival. She smiled at them, not minding that their delight was caused by the things she'd brought with her.

The land to the east of the castle, being so near to the sea and ravaged by its salt gales, was the most unproductive on the estate. The cottagers who lived there barely scraped a living during the best of times.

'I hear that you've a new brother.'

She searched in her bundle and gave them each a sweetmeat before following them into the cottage where she made her way to where their mother lay.

'How are you, Agnes?'

She gave her the parcel and marvelled at how well the woman looked. This was her fourth child. Not all women died in childbirth. She had to remember that.

After admiring the baby and promising she'd return soon, Elinor left, and after a brisk gallop they came to Erthwain harbour. It was one of the prettiest parts of her land but, to her mind, it was also the weakest. Her father had often spoken about fortifying the headland, and it would have been her first act if she'd been William. She gave a deep sigh. Everything always came back to him. Without his consent, she was powerless to do anything.

They began their return journey, the soldiers close by and fully alert as they were near Guy de Riddington's estates.

She often came this way but today unease prickled the fine hairs at the back of her neck. Even Fleur was skittish and needed careful handling.

It happened almost immediately. The captain gave the command and the others encircled her, their swords drawn. What was the danger? Elinor's heart thundered in her breast. She hadn't seen anything. When she found her voice, she turned to the nearest man.

'What is it?'

His gaze remained fixed ahead.

'Maybe a trap, Lady Elinor.'

Her fingers tightened around the dagger at her waist. The first who attempted to take her would be surprised that she knew how to use it. It was the one thing Gilbert had taught her. They remained unmoving for several moments.

'What did you see?' she demanded of the captain when she could bear it no longer.

'That.'

He pointed a little distance ahead.

'What?'

She couldn't see anything until she urged Fleur forward and the circle opened slightly to allow her a view.

'A dead man?'

Alarm juddered through her body as she saw blood on the ground beside the still figure.

'Maybe he is and maybe he isn't,' the guard murmured.

'Then I bid you find out.'

Dislike was thinly veiled as the man dismounted from the safety of his mount, but he nevertheless obeyed her command. He positioned his sword at the man's neck and gave him a hefty kick.

'Not like that!' she shouted, as the wretch moaned loudly.

'Seems he's still alive.'

Elinor slid from her saddle and walked towards them.

'This is no trap. Whoever attacked him and left him for dead wouldn't risk remaining here and being hanged for a murder.'

The men-at-arms gave her passage but maintained their guard.

'Turn him,' she commanded. 'Gently!'

She gazed at the deep gash on the man's right arm.

'A sword wound?'

She glanced up at the soldier, who nodded in confirmation. There were other blade cuts about his body but this was the one, despite it being near no major organs, that would prove to be fatal.

'He's lost a lot of blood,' she whispered.

'Aye, he won't last long.'

Elinor used her dagger to cut two long strips from the bottom of her shift. The first, she pressed over the wound and the second, she bound tightly around it. Her task was hampered by the fact that he smelled more foul than the castle moat in high summer and she had to pause every few moments to gulp in sweeter air.

'We need to get him back to the castle.'

The man-at-arms sucked his teeth.

'Send a cart back for him,' she snapped.

She considered the ashen pallor of the wounded man just visible under the tangled mass of filthy hair and beard.

'He'd be dead before it got here.'

The soldier's expression didn't change.

'He'll be dead before long anyway.'

'Perhaps I can save him.'

He wasn't one of her servants, but he'd been attacked on her land and she felt a responsibility towards him. She wouldn't wager on his chances but she had to try to save his life.

'One of you must ride with him before you,' she declared, and there was immediate dissent.

She looked to the captain but he refused to meet her eyes.

'Very well, then, I shall choose.'

She pointed to one of them.

'You. I want you to carry this man on your horse and treat him as carefully as if he were your own brother.'

The soldier shook his head.

'Nay, my lady. Send a cart for him. He's ranker than a dung heap.'

Her heart skipped a beat. She knew that William's men held her in little regard but this was the first time one of them had openly disobeyed her. What was she to do? She looked to Robert but he looked away. So what would her father have done now? What would the brute who had been her brother have done?

She took a breath to still her nerves, and pretended an arrogance she was far from feeling as she gazed up at the man.

'As you wish, but be prepared for the flogging that awaits you at the castle on your return.'

The soldier laughed nervously, but she ignored him and turned her attention to the others.

'Do you all refuse me? Will I give the order to have you all flogged?'

Every soldier dismounted. None rushed to pick up the wounded man but each was ready to if she asked. She glanced coldly at her first choice and prayed he'd now obey her command. She'd never ordered a flogging in her life and hoped she never would.

'Forgive me, my lady.' He inclined his head in a bow. 'I'll take him on my horse if you'll allow it.'

'As carefully as if he were your brother,' she reminded him.

He hesitated and she wondered if he were even now going to refuse.

'Well?'

The man gave her a sly look.

'I don't care overmuch for my brother, Lady Elinor.'

She smiled, and the tension between them lifted.

'As carefully as if he were your father?'

He slid an arm under the wounded man's neck.

'Aye, I liked my father well enough.'

'Help him.'

She directed the request to the other soldiers, and between them the man was lifted and half supported by the horse's neck. His eyes flickered open.

'Who are you? Who did this to you? What are you doing here?'

Her questions met no response bar a smile that was oddly familiar. Perhaps he was a pedlar who had once traded at the castle and been forced by hard times into beggary. But if he were conscious his chances of survival were greater. She gripped his left hand and placed it over the wound.

'Press hard,' she urged him. 'You have lost a lot of blood.'

Again he smiled, and her heart sank. A dying man who no longer felt pain had often passed the threshold from which there was no return . . .

William de Valences closed his eyes and knew that he'd left all his earthly cares behind. He'd arrived in heaven, and it was a source of some consolation that the angel who greeted him bore the face of his wife.

3

Elinor started in surprise when the wretch lying on the ground of the outer bailey said her name. She raised her hand to prevent a soldier kicking him for his impudence.

'What shall we do with him?' the man asked instead.

'Elinor,' he sighed once again.

It had been in her mind to have him taken to the stables. It was warm and the horses wouldn't take offence at his smell, but it was also close to the drawbridge. Anyone who entered the castle could gain entry there. Someone wanted this man dead, and it would be the matter of a moment to complete the deed.

'Take him to Lord Gilbert's chamber,' she said as they entered the courtyard.

'My lady!'

She pierced him with one glance.

'Do I need to explain my actions to you?'

He bent to do her bidding but she saw the look that flashed between the guards. She would have to be careful. A lord, providing he was a strong one, could be as mad as he liked. A lady could not.

Meg had come close, her eyes as wide as a fully-waxed moon.

'Lord Gilbert's chamber?' she whispered.

Elinor shrugged.

'Gilbert would have left him at the side of the road. If he'd been in his path he'd have ridden over him. Perhaps it'll benefit his soul to do some good after his death.'

Once in the room, Elinor gazed at the wretch lying in her brother's bed. How should she treat him? It was one thing sprinkling dried comfrey root on a cut. It was quite another dealing with a dying man. Perhaps she'd do him better service by calling for a priest to tend his soul. The wound was deep. Once it had been cleaned it would have to be sewn. Should she save him the suffering and allow him to pass away peacefully?

She shook herself. Who was she to decide such matters? She must do her best and trust to the Almighty for the rest.

'Agrimony and meadow cranesbill mashed into a poultice,' she muttered.

Hopefully they had ample supplies of poppy juice because, even if he survived, the wound fever would set in soon.

★ ★ ★

The fires of hell crackled around him, but its flames couldn't consume him while the angel with the face of his wife ministered to his needs. He gulped greedily at the liquid she gave him, liquid that offered oblivion and free-dom from pain.

'Elinor.'

He smiled his thanks as she pressed a

cool cloth over his forehead. He closed his eyes and drifted back to oblivion.

It might have been the next day, it might have been the next week, when he opened his eyes, while she was urging him to drink. He spat the foul brew on to the floor.

'Poppy juice and valerian,' he grumbled. 'You won't poison me with your potions.'

'What did you say?'

He looked at her blankly. What had he said? He no longer recalled.

'Who are you?' she asked.

The same question, he thought, over and over again.

'Why do you keep asking?' he shouted, and immediately regretted raising his voice, both for the effect on his wife and for the pain that racked his skull.

The fear he read in her eyes was short-lived, replaced by an anger that scorched him.

'If I hadn't brought you to the castle, you'd be dead. If I hadn't tended and stitched your wounds, you'd be dead. If

I hadn't nursed you and gone without rest, you'd be dead. And if I hadn't fed you this foul brew, you would most certainly be dead. Only one question have I asked you. I believe that you owe me the answer.'

'Forgive me.'

During the weeks he'd lived in the woods by order of the king, he'd worried how his new wife would manage in his absence. He needn't have done. The woman he'd married was as strong as any man. He gazed up at the face that had looked down at him kindly through his illness. When he'd first seen her, he hadn't thought her over-pretty. How wrong he'd been. She was beautiful.

'I'll forgive you when you tell me your name,' she replied.

'You don't know?'

The reason for her continually asking it was finally answered.

'You've tended me all this time and you don't know?'

Her fingers clenched with frustration.

'Tell me now or I shall have you removed to the stables where whoever did this can finish you off for certain.'

'I shall remain here.'

He scratched at the beard covering his face and desired with all his heart to remove it. Yet it had served him well. His companions hadn't been jesting when they said his own mother would have cast him aside as a beggar.

'You are very bold. I'll ask you for the last time. Who are you?'

He rested his head more comfortably against the pillow.

'Think on't, Elinor. You know the answer.'

Colour drained from her face.

'No, it can't be,' she gasped, and looked to him for answer.

'Good morrow, wife,' he said, and she burst into tears.

He reached out to comfort her but she swept him aside.

'You!' she screeched. 'You? If I'd known it was you, I'd have left you for the foxes!'

'Elinor?'

He hadn't reckoned on such a reaction and readied himself for attack. She was shaking with rage and her pallor had been replaced by a crimson hue. She picked up the cup and flung the contents at him before storming to the door.

'Come back!'

Her reply was unfit for anywhere other than a guardroom!

'I order you to come back!' he shouted, but she was gone.

Her lungs protested as she ran up the twisting steps to the battlements, and they were almost bursting as she grasped the crenellated stone at the top and gulped in mouthfuls of air. What a fool she was! How could she have nursed him and not known that he was her husband?

What game had he been playing? Granted, it had almost been the end of him, but game it had been nevertheless, and he'd chosen to play it rather than take his place at her side. Did he know what she'd suffered these many weeks? The sly glances, sympathy and amusement of everyone towards a wife whose husband found her so distasteful on their wedding night that he'd left the next morning and never returned?

She hated him. She let out a sob, and one of the guards turned to give her a curious look.

No, she didn't hate him. She remembered how he'd stirred emotions in her that she had never felt before, and even on their wedding night, when she had shamed herself, he had shown understanding.

But she didn't understand him, couldn't understand why he'd never come back to her, and why he'd allowed his hair to grow so long and his clothes so filthy that his own men were ready to defy her rather than carry him back to the castle.

Her sigh was lost on the wind. She gulped in the breath that was lost before returning to her brother's chamber. So her lord was back. How often had she wished it these past months? And now that he was, she'd screamed at him that she wished he was dead. He'd ordered her to stay and she'd disobeyed him. If she'd lost her temper with Gilbert in such a way, he'd have beaten and starved her for a week. She had to return and apologise.

At the door of the chamber, she paused to remind herself to be a meek and dutiful wife, but all such thoughts vanished at the sight that greeted her within.

'What in the name of heaven do you think you're doing?' she screeched.

Had she tended his wounds and nursed him through fever and delirium to have him expire now? Fresh blood seeped through the linen dressings, caused, no doubt, by the effort of opening the huge oak chest in the corner of the room. He'd fallen and was clawing himself upright. William's cold gaze swept over her.

'Help me.'

But she was already rushing to his aid

before he'd issued the command.

'What do you think you're doing?' she asked again, as he leaned heavily against her.

His response was lightning swift. In one deft movement, he extracted the dagger from her waist and pulled her to him.

'I was searching for weapons, and now I have one.'

'And much good it'll do you.'

His arm wavered with the effort of holding it.

'If you're of a mind to slit my throat then you'd better do it quickly before you fall down again.'

'I've no wish to hurt you,' the answer came.

'Then let me help you back to bed.'

'I am a soldier and will face my enemies standing upright. I will not be slain in bed.'

'You won't be upright much longer.'

His weight grew heavier and heavier as he leaned against her shoulder.

'Where did you go? Whom did you

tell?' he demanded.

'I told no-one. Now let me help you back to bed. You are my lord and I'll allow no harm to befall you.'

He was slipping in and out of unconsciousness by the time she managed to lay him between the sheets and bent to remove the dagger in case he should do himself injury. Despite his weakness, the grip on its hilt was firm, and he refused to yield it. What foolhardiness had caused him to leap out of bed and undo all the healing that had taken place over the past week?

Her lips compressed as she saw the red stains on the clean linen dressings. She sighed and turned away, but a noise like the shifting of sand turned her back. His eyes were closed. There was no-one else in the room. With trembling hands, she crossed herself before turning away again. This time the noise was more recognisable as a human voice.

'My lord?' She brought her face close to his.

'Bring me a sword,' he commanded.

How he would find the strength to wield it she couldn't imagine, but he wouldn't settle until she'd taken Gilbert's sword from the chest and placed it at his side.

After he'd rested, she smeared ointment over his wound and studied it with a critical eye.

'I had done good work with my needle, but now the stitching is like to look clumsy. I'd be pleased if you didn't get up again.'

His clear gaze rested on her face a moment, but he made no promise.

'Who else knows I'm here?' he asked again.

'No-one.'

'Your maidservant?'

'No.'

'It is well. Then who do they think I am?'

'A beggar.'

'And who did you think I was?'

'The same.'

His eyebrows disappeared into the thick tangle of his hair.

'You would tend a beggar's wounds in your brother's chamber?'

'Yes.'

He stared at her, disbelieving.

'And what have people said about such a thing?'

'They haven't said anything to me. They've probably forgotten you're here.'

'And the guards?'

'Nothing. Since I threatened to have them flogged they are more careful what they say to me.'

He looked at her sharply but said nothing.

'Now rest, and I shall return with some food.'

'Elinor.'

She turned back.

'Not a word to anyone about my presence here,' he reminded her.

She glared at him. Hadn't she already said so?

'You've told me this already and I understood it the first time! Would you like me to sink to my knees and swear it?'

His hand formed into a fist and his expression darkened.

'A word from me, wife, and you could spend the rest of your days locked in the solar. Is that what you want?'

Her eyes widened as she took in his threat. What was wrong with her? She knew he had the power to do it, so what devil in her sought to provoke him? She sank to her knees.

'I beg your pardon, Lord William. I'm prepared to swear an oath that I will not betray you to anyone.'

'Get up, Elinor.'

His voice was weary as he motioned her to rise.

'Your word to me is sufficient.'

William lay back on the bed and cursed the weakness that made him lose his temper with his wife. Lock her up for the rest of her life? He didn't want to beat her into submission. It wasn't submission he wanted. He wanted her love. He groaned. Perhaps it was the effects of the fever. For day after day, her face had floated above him like an angel. She was protecting him and nursing him back to health. It was this presence he was beginning to fall in love with. It had been a shock like no other when she'd spat out her hate.

'If I'd known it was you, I'd have left you for the foxes,' she'd screamed, and the words had haunted him ever since.

It was those words that had caused his loss of temper. Why did she hate him so? He'd caused her no harm. Yet she'd made herself unconscious on their wedding night rather than face his attentions. He'd already forgiven her, believing it to be maidenly modesty. But what if there was another reason? Could she have promised her heart to another? Was that why she wanted him dead?

But who? The steward? William thought a moment before giving a snort of self disgust. What was he thinking? The man was as upright and loyal as any he'd encountered. He must stop this.

Then it came to him. The man he'd seen riding with his wife when he'd been hiding in the woods, who'd also been there on the day she'd found him wounded — Robert Latimer. He was of the mould that women found attractive, hair the colour of ripening corn and a smile that could charm.

What else did he know about him? Knight? No, he was page to the old lord and then squire, and of a similar age to Elinor. They must have played together as children.

Did they play together still? He slanted a deeply suspicious glance at his wife as she entered the chamber. She sank into a deep curtsey. It was a submissive act, yet there was nothing remotely submissive about the fire that glinted in her hastily-lowered lids.

'Did I ask you to do that?'

She kept her eyes lowered.

'I wished to demonstrate that I am an obedient wife, my lord. I've no wish to spend my days locked in the solar.'

He hissed in his breath as her words

twisted in his gut. Women might be frailer than men but they could find their opponent's weakness and thrust in the blade as skilfully as any warrior.

'Get up, Elinor.'

'Yes, my lord.'

'William! My given name is William!'

Her eyes flickered with thinly-veiled hostility. Fear, shock, anger, contempt — all of these he'd read there. Only when she hadn't known who he was had he seen any tenderness. Tenderness to a beggar! Hate to a husband! What had he done to deserve such?

'I recall asking you to call me by my given name when we were alone. Had you forgotten?'

'No.'

She twined her fingers together, battling with feelings he could only guess at. Did the name Robert come more easily to her lips? Was that the name she'd hoped for her husband?

Elinor winced. What did this man want from her? In trying to demonstrate her obedience, she'd only succeeded in annoying him. And why did he stare at her so coldly, as if she'd tried to murder him? He owed his life to her.

Was that it? Did his pride rebel at being indebted to a woman?

'I've spoken to the guard and given instructions for this part of the castle to be guarded only by my own men. It can be arranged without drawing suspicion, so you may rest easy as to my safety,' he was saying.

'You think I'd have had you murdered in your bed?'

It slipped out before she could snap her mouth closed. Curse her tongue! She jabbed her nails deep into her palms and waited for punishment.

'Elinor?'

'I beg your forgiveness, William,' she whispered.

'You have it.'

The shock was so great that her gaze shot upwards, to be captured immediately by the assessing eyes levelled in her direction.

'I confess I prefer your true thoughts

to the sham of your obedience.'

A guilty heat crept over her cheeks.

He shrugged. 'It is a personal taste. After a life spent at court, I find it refreshing.'

'I see.'

'I'm not sure you do. When we're not alone, I caution you to curb your tongue. I won't have it said that I'm unable to control my wife.'

For twenty years she'd been learning to curb her tongue in public. Surely it shouldn't be difficult to continue.

'Your friends will envy you your most dutiful wife, William.'

'Then I am truly blessed.'

She wondered if he mocked her, but his face told her nothing. One reason for this might be the hair that obscured it.

'You will want to cut your hair and remove your beard,' she began. 'I'll bring water and — '

'You will not.'

She clamped her mouth closed. If Lord William de Valances wished to wear his hair thus then it wouldn't be she that informed him he looked disgusting. He scratched his beard.

'Don't you like me like this, wife?'

Her lips tightened.

'My lord may wear his hair in any fashion he chooses.'

'That's not what I asked.' He gave that strange half-smile of his. 'I'm teasing you, Elinor. Have you never been teased before?'

'My brother was fond of teasing me.'

'But you didn't care for it?'

Gilbert's teasing took the form of finding out what she most desired and denying her it. If she already possessed it then he delighted in taking it from her.

'No, William, I wasn't over-fond of being teased by him.'

His smile faded. 'I'll leave my hair as it is until I am stronger. If I'm seen, I'm unlikely to be recognised.'

She nodded. 'I understand.'

'But I will require water for washing after I have eaten.'

'I will arrange it.'

She was at the door when he spoke. 'There is one more matter, Elinor.'

She groaned.

'I know. Not a word to anyone about your presence here. I'm not likely to forget.'

' 'Twas not that.' Again the half-smile. 'I wished to thank you for saving my life.'

4

This woman would never bore him. The thought surprised him, as did the crimson staining her cheekbones as she helped him bathe. What a curious mixture of confidence and uncertainty she was, one moment scolding him to keep his wound dry, the next averting her eyes to avoid his nakedness.

Women were clever, taught, it seemed, from the cradle in ways to fool their men folk. He, like most men, had been duped by their wiles, but he couldn't believe this was a sham. His suspicions about her had been misplaced.

He gave a deep groan and closed his eyes as the warm water caressed his lower limbs. Pleasure. It had been in precious short supply these past months, and he accepted it gratefully. A soothing warmth flowed into his right arm as his wife washed carefully around the wound. With a skill honed by hunting, he could distinguish her scent with his eyes closed — the smell of her long auburn hair worn in a thick plait down her back, the perfume that rose from her gown as she moved around him with shy grace, and the heated essence of her skin when it flushed with embarrassment or anger. Oh, how he wanted her!

'Does the wound pain you, William?'

She paused in her ministrations as his muscles tensed.

'No. Pray continue.'

Her fingertips hovered uncertainly over his arm and he craved their touch.

She did as she was bid, and he watched as she carried out the task. Her hands were small. He could crush both of them easily in one fist, yet they displayed a dexterity and skill that belied their fragility. Her body, too, was fine and delicate, as white as the snow of winter. Neither blemish nor scar tainted its perfection.

What a different bundle of flesh he

was! He could trace his progress from boyhood to man by the marks they'd left on the journey. He glanced at the scars that wound a silvery trail over his body. Once healed, he'd paid them little heed. They'd become as familiar to him as his fingers and toes. But what of her? Did the sight of him repulse her? He'd wager that Robert Latimer's body was as perfect as the day he was born, that he'd never felt the gut-churning thud of metal against bone as an opponent's sword found its mark.

With a muttered curse, he plunged his head under the water and shook it about to remove the dirt. When he came up again, she was waiting with a jug of perfumed water.

'Shall I?' Her voice was hesitant.

He nodded, and tipped his head back so that she could pour the fragrant liquid through his hair. As she did so, her fingers twisted through the strands, untangling knots and affecting a pleasant massage of his scalp. It was almost worth the nuisance of wearing his hair longer to have her provide this service for him.

'Oh,' she gasped.

The pleasure ceased abruptly, and he opened one eye in irritation. She probed his head and an old pain protested its awakening.

'You have a great ridge along here.'

'The blade of a battleaxe which sought to cleave my skull in two. Its owner no longer breathes.'

He rose to his feet and snatched the drying cloth from her hands. Immediately she averted her eyes, but on this occasion it annoyed rather than amused him.

'I am a warrior, Elinor. What do you expect?'

His harsh words reverberated in her brain as she helped him to bed. She didn't know how she'd angered him. He'd seemed to be enjoying his bath, and she, too, had been enjoying becoming acquainted with this strange male body.

When he asserted his right as a

husband, she knew this body would cause her some pain. But today, although she felt its strength beneath her fingertips, it didn't threaten her. With his wide shoulders, muscular torso and long, powerful limbs, she found William de Valences beautiful.

The next day, when they broke their fast together, he announced, 'I believe I shall dress today. Do you think that is well?'

She knew he'd do exactly as he wanted but was pleased that he'd thought to consider her.

'Shall you dress in your own clothes?'

'No. I bid you bring me peasant's clothes, but clean ones, if you please.'

He sipped the ale and gazed at the ornately-carved bedposts hung with richly-coloured brocade and silk.

'This is a fine bed.'

'Yes. Gilbert was never one to deny himself any comfort.'

'Shall we take it for ours?'

'No!'

He gave her a quizzical look.

'I would rather not, William, if it pleases you,' she added in a quieter tone.

'So be it.'

He gazed at her, a strange, smouldering gaze.

'I would hope that we can please each other, wife.'

'Yes.'

She bent to refill his cup and, in her confusion, spilled some of it over his hand. Without comment, he lifted it to his mouth and licked the spillage without taking his eyes from hers.

'I met your brother several times. I was present at the tourney when he died.'

'My father never recovered from the loss,' she said flatly.

'But you did?'

'Yes.'

She stared back at him, not pretending a grief she'd never felt. He maintained her gaze, his expression thoughtful.

'Our situations are not unlike. I knew

that I'd never hold the lands on which I was born. I wager you never expected to hold such power.'

What power? Did he believe her dislike of Gilbert was caused by jealousy?

'I never desired this.'

'I did.'

Both his honestly and the smile that accompanied it were disarming.

'I didn't.'

'You'd have preferred, perhaps, to have been born a serf and eke out your existence as such?'

'Maybe I'd have preferred to have been born a man,' she retaliated.

He burst out laughing.

'I was teasing you, Elinor. I forgot that you weren't over-fond of the game.'

To hide her flaming cheeks, she bent to untie the linen covering his wound.

'It will need fresh ointment.'

'Let it be. It is well.'

He snatched her arm away but remained smiling.

'So, my lady wife wishes she were

born a man. That's something no woman's ever said to me. I also attended the joust that your father held here.'

'I remember you.'

She wasn't likely to forget the knight who had claimed the main prize money, the knight whom every woman there had been urging on to victory.

'You were there?' His eyebrows rose in surprise.

'Yes, I was there. My father had me dressed in the finest clothes coin could buy so that I might attract a husband.'

His smile faded to an expression of sympathy.

'But you didn't?'

'Oh, yes, I did, but he'd already been on this earth for fifty years. I cried continually for three whole days and nights until my father lost patience and sent him away.'

William hid his amusement behind his hand.

'And what if I had offered for you?'

'Maybe I'd have only cried for two.'

His laughter rang around the room.

'I wish I remembered you, but I confess that I don't.'

'I wouldn't have interested you then. The lands that my father settled on me weren't vast.'

To her surprise he reached out and took her hand, then surprised her even more by stroking gently around the palm of it with his thumb.

'I wasn't seeking a wife at that time, Elinor. All that concerned me was winning the joust in order to pay my men and survive at court.'

She stood up, strangely affected by the sensation of his touch.

'I'll bring you the clothes you requested, and then I should go riding.'

'Would you rather go riding than stay and talk to me?'

'I'll stay if you wish, William, but it will draw suspicion. I ride out every morning at this time.'

He shrugged.

'Then go. I'll have to become acquainted with my wife some other time.'

★　★　★

The sweat stood on his brow as he pulled on his breeches. He should have accepted Elinor's offer of help but pride had prevented him. The room spun like a child's top and he fell to the floor. The animal pelts there were a softer mattress than many he'd lain on. He closed his eyes and waited until he had strength to move.

He could call the guard. He was a man he trusted, but he couldn't bear anyone to witness his weakness. A leader should be strong. A husband should be strong. He wished more than anything that it hadn't been his wife who'd come across him lying in the dirt. And yet if she hadn't, he wouldn't be in her brother's chamber at this moment. He twisted to his side, grabbed the thick wooden bed leg and pulled himself upright.

What use had it all been? He'd been so close to proving Guy de Riddington's treachery and fulfilling his promise to the king before he'd been discovered and left for dead. Thankfully, those who'd thought to deprive him of life hadn't realised his true identity or they'd have made certain to accomplish the deed. His head would even now be decorating a pole for de Riddington's amusement.

Now what? Long acquaintance with Henry had taught him that the king wasn't interested in reasons or excuses. All he cared for were results. He'd allowed William a few weeks' grace on account of his illness, but he wanted Guy de Riddington. He wanted proof that he was conspiring with Robert in France to topple him from his throne.

Self-pity didn't sit easily on William, and it soon toppled off as his strength returned. His wife was right. He must be careful not to tire himself and undo her work.

His wife. He repeated the words and smiled to himself. Henry had driven a hard bargain with her as the prize, but he was beginning to believe that she might be worth the cost. He enjoyed talking to her. That was a surprise, for conversation was the last thing he'd ever looked for in a woman. He lay on the bed and realised that he wanted to know everything about her . . .

How long had he slept? This cursed weakness made him easy game for any with a mind to murder him, and there was a traitor in this household. That much he had discovered. He thrust the covers away and, before his strength failed again, pulled on the homespun tunic and called for the guard.

Where was his wife? Had she returned safely from her ride? The guard reassured him.

'Lady Elinor returned some time ago, my lord. Shall I send word that you desire her presence?'

'No.'

He didn't want to chance anyone's suspicions by summoning her. His presence here had to remain a secret. He dismissed the man and turned his attention to what was happening outside his window. Beyond the castle walls the harvest had been gathered in and the earth was resting. It was a fine view. He wondered how often Gilbert of Elleston had stood here appreciating it like him. He hadn't liked the man, but he had to admire his choice of bedchamber. Apart from the battlements, it was probably the best vantage point in the castle.

Ignoring the pain in his side, he made his way to the door. Immediately outside, a narrow arrow slit afforded a view over the garrison. Excellent. He presumed that the stone steps beside it led down to the great hall, but he hadn't the strength to confirm it. To his right was a short gallery, at the end of which the guard had his post. Dismissing the man's offer of help, he walked along and, careful not to be seen from below, looked down into the great hall.

Blessed with the vision of a hawk, he could view everything that was happening below without anyone seeing him. If the person passing information to Guy de Riddington was here, he was well placed to catch him, but for now, the hall was relatively quiet. Servants awaited the order to bring out the trestles and lay them for dinner and in the meantime occupied themselves according to age. The younger men indulged in horseplay to impress the serving girls, while the older of both sexes remained around the fire and warmed their bones.

His recent hardships forgotten, William watched the young men's antics. As a young squire, desperate for the women to like him, he'd behaved exactly the same. His lips curved in amusement when one brave soul tried to steal a kiss and received a sound blow to the head for his pains.

His gaze travelled along the hall to its farthest end where the dais stood. It was empty, as he expected it to be, but the room leading from it was not. Elinor! The breath caught in his throat as he recognised his wife. The reaction surprised him. She had a simple rather than a great beauty. In contrast to some at court she was almost plain, yet there was a harmony about her face and figure that sparked his desire and made the blood flow quicker through his veins.

There was something different about her that he hadn't seen before. She was laughing! Her face was flushed and her eyes were sparkling. William stepped back. Just who had provoked such merriment in his wife?

Robert Latimer! Surprise was slight, though not the anger that twisted his gut at having his suspicions confirmed. Did she have no shame? They were sitting so close they were almost touching. How long had this been going on? Was his wife still pure? By God and all the saints, he'd never have entered into this marriage bargain if he'd had the slightest suspicion she wasn't!

His vision tilted as a wave of nausea swept over him, and the two bodies of Elinor and Latimer seemed to merge into one for one mocking instant. He held grimly on to the stone ledge until he could again see clearly, and still they were together, not merged, but as close as made little difference, unaware or totally indifferent to any who might observe them.

No-one in the hall paid them any heed. Had this happened in his absence or was such closeness common before his arrival? His head spun with trying to unravel the truth. Had he spent too long embroiled in the intrigues of court? Perhaps this was simply youthful friendship allowed to grow unchecked, and it attracted little attention because it had always been so. His wife was innocent and he was cynical beyond his years for not accepting it. But still he continued to watch, though the sight of them together festered like an unclean wound. If he'd had the strength he'd have confronted them, but this cursed weakness only added to his frustration.

With an almighty effort he tore his gaze away. He despised himself for spying on her like this. What purpose did it serve? Or course she was pure.

She wouldn't dare to be otherwise. It was her part of the bargain. And then he heard her laugh. It was such a joyful, musical sound that he had to look down to where she sat smiling at Latimer, who ducked his head in a movement that appeared to be a kiss. Was it a kiss? He couldn't be certain from his angle of vision.

Of course it hadn't been a kiss! Every shred of reason told him that a man wouldn't kiss another man's wife in full view of everyone. If he were that arrogant then he fully deserved to die. In his mind's eye, he saw his rival equipped to fight him. Long experience had taught that the unlikeliest of men could find great courage in battle, but Robert Latimer wasn't one of them. He'd stake his life on it.

Groaning, he shook his head to chase away such thoughts. He must return to his bed. Fever still gripped his body judging by the strange visions that churned through his brain. Perhaps he was imagining everything. He made to move, but there was nothing imaginary about what he witnessed next. Latimer reached over and covered her hand with his.

For several long moments, William forgot to breathe. If she pulled her hand away he would forgive her. He would probably kill Latimer, but he would forgive her, but she didn't. Unresisting, she allowed his hand to remain where it was.

Strength fuelled by rage flooded his body. He sped along the gallery and would have gone down the steps to the great hall if the steps hadn't rushed to greet him first. And then he was falling, deeper and deeper into a swirling chasm, and then there was only blackness.

*　*　*

'He's awake, my lady.'

Elinor uttered a prayer of thanks closely followed by a groan of disbelief when she saw it wasn't yet light outside.

She'd sat at William's bedside half the night and her head felt as though it were stuffed with wool. Meg held out her gown.

'Why you concern yourself with the health of a beggar is beyond my reckoning.'

Wearily, Elinor accepted her help.

'Have you heard of Christian charity?'

'Christian charity! Pah! I'd give him Christian charity if it was up to me. I'd tell him to find it with the monks! Ungrateful wretch!'

'Whatever is the matter, Meg?'

'That filthy beggar! 'Fetch your mistress!' he said to me as if he were the king himself, and with a look that'd sour milk. 'You can fetch her yourself if you take that tone with me,' I says to him, and I'd have said a lot more besides if he hadn't fixed me a look as if he'd murder me where I stood.'

Her head throbbing, Elinor reached for her cloak and was grateful for its fur lining as she wrapped it tightly around herself for warmth. What was William thinking of? He must have decided that acting the beggar wasn't to his taste any more, but this was no way to treat her most loyal servant.

'I'll speak to him.' She laid a hand on Meg's shoulder. 'Now get some sleep.'

Meg bent to pull out the truckle bed but Elinor stopped her.

'My sheets are still warm. One of us may as well have the benefit.'

Meg climbed into the bed but couldn't resist one last retort.

'There I was thinking that only beggars had hopes of receiving such goodness.'

While the rest of the castle slept, Elinor made her way to her husband's room. At least now she would find out why he'd fallen down the steps. Had he been fleeing from the guard on duty or had he been pushed? She'd discovered nothing from the man himself.

William was sitting up in bed, but not even the faint candlelight hid the blackness of his expression. She felt a moment of terror as the flickering light cast strange shadows over his face, causing him to look more like a devil than a human being, a devil who hated her.

Taking a breath, she pushed away her fear and entered the room. Of course he didn't hate her. He was her husband.

'I am glad to see you recovered, William.'

'Of course you are,' he snarled.

'Of course I am,' she repeated, glad that her voice sounder steadier than she felt. 'I was worried about you.'

'Indeed?' His countenance grew ever darker.

'Yes, indeed.'

What was the matter with him? Didn't he know she'd sat with him most of the night? Judging from the blackness of his look, he probably didn't. She took a breath before attempting to explain.

'I'm sorry that — '

'Where is Roger Fitzhugh?'

She stared at him blankly.

'The man who was on duty here,' he elaborated.

'Locked in the dungeon until I find out what happened to you.'

His fist tightened on the bedclothes.

'That's what they told me, but I had to hear it from your own lips. How dare you, Elinor, throw one of my most trusted men into a cell?'

'I dare because of you! Because your safety was the most important thing to me!'

'Hah! Didn't I tell you, didn't I make it plain, that I'd be guarded only by men I'd trusted with my life?'

'You were lying halfway down the steps, your head in a pool of blood. The man had no explanation other than you'd fallen. What was I supposed to do?'

'You were supposed to believe him.'

'William, how many times have you told me to keep your presence here secret? Why should you take it into your head to go down the steps to the great hall?'

His eyes flickered away from hers.

'I had my reasons,' he replied in hushed tones.

'You weren't pushed?'

'No.'

She stared at his handsome, obstinate face, and felt a surge of anger such as she'd never felt. How dare he frighten her so badly yesterday?

'No-one was threatening to harm you? No-one was chasing you?' she clarified.

'No.'

'You got out of bed and went down the steps yourself?'

'I have said as much.'

'Then you are a fool without not even the sense of a beast of the field. An animal will lie low when ill. It has the sense not to move around until its wounds have healed, the sense not to do itself further harm.'

'Have you quite finished?'

She should have heeded the savage glint in his eye.

'No, I haven't,' she began, but he

stopped her in mid-flow.

'You'll curb your tongue, wife. Give me some peace. Would you have me punish you as a scold?'

The rest of her words died instantly on her lips as she stared at him with shock. What monster was this who lay in her brother's bed? Even as she thought it, she knew the answer. This was a monster who held complete domination over her. He could arrange for her to take Roger Fitzhugh's place in the dungeon, and make her wear the cruellest of contraptions devised to silence a woman. To her chagrin she began to shake, and dropped into a low curtsey to disguise her fear.

'I beg your pardon, William. Please believe that worry for your safety was my only concern. But I have been remiss in my duties. Let me bring food and drink to break your fast.'

And before he could say anything, she gathered up her gown and escaped the room.

Slowly, rhythmically, William brought

his head back and thudded it against the richly-carved headboard. What was it about this woman that made him behave so? He recalled how she'd trembled with fear, and he cursed fluently. In his experience, all bullies were cowards. So what did that make him? Once more his head pounded the headboard. In all his years, he'd never had occasion to despise himself so thoroughly.

'My lord?'

He had to gain control of himself before she came back or he was likely to lash out at her again. Though her words stung like poisoned barbs he should have curbed his own tongue. After all, what she'd said had been true. He had been a madman to attempt the steps. Two months in hiding, two months living like an animal would all have been wasted if he'd appeared in the great hall. Then he remembered why he'd acted so foolishly — the young cur sniffing around his wife! That hadn't been imagination.

He heard the tread of feet on the steps and composed his features. He couldn't do anything about if for the present. He couldn't allow it to interfere with his plans. He was so close to fulfilling his bargain to King Henry.

Elinor stepped hesitantly into the room. He studied her pale, frightened face and forced himself to believe in her until he could prove otherwise. His body had always been quick to heal. It wouldn't be long before he had the strength to demand that which was legally his, and then he would know for certain where her loyalty lay.

5

Elinor narrowly avoided pouring more ale into his already overflowing cup as he spoke to her once she'd entered the room. There was no change of expression in the cold eyes staring into her soul but she knew that he registered everything. She was more nervous now than she'd been on her wedding night and, not for the first time, regretted swallowing the draught of poppy juice and valerian. Feminine instinct told her that if she hadn't done so, she'd be a lot easier with her husband now.

'How was the harvest?' he asked.

Why did she feel that everything he said to her had a hidden meaning?

'Do you desire the steward to be brought before you?' she asked, and irritation flashed across his brow.

'I do not.'

He bent to sip at his over-full cup.

'You reply to my question with another question. Do you think that you could make another attempt at answering it?'

'I'm sorry, William, I don't know the figures, but it was a good harvest,' she faltered.

'It was a good harvest. Thank you. That was all the answer I hoped for.'

She drew a breath of relief as he turned his attention to the fish on his plate. Was that it? Had simple curiosity been the motive for his question? She couldn't believe it. There was nothing simple about this man.

As he ate, her mind drifted back to the previous month. It had been a good harvest. The people had toiled in the fields until the last night, and the feast she'd ordered for them at the end of it had demonstrated her thanks in equal measure. Was that the purpose behind his question? Did he wish her to know that he was aware of her generosity to the peasants and disapproved of it? She gave a deep sigh and chewed at her lip.

If that was so then why didn't he say as much instead of hinting at it?

'What?' he asked suddenly.

'I didn't say anything.'

'I'd like to know what you wished to say to me.'

'Nothing.' She wouldn't be drawn into an argument and rebuked again.

'Nothing?'

She shook her head.

'Then it is a nothing that is desperate to escape, a nothing that forces you to bite on your lips rather than let it forth,' he said cuttingly.

Elinor glared at him.

'My lord has told me to curb my tongue. Does he now object when he witnesses me doing just that?'

His reaction was totally unexpected. With an oath, he brought his head back and slammed it into the headboard. She stared at him, not daring to move, not daring to point out the folly of his action considering the head wound he had only recently sustained.

He closed his eyes and she saw the

pain bead on his brow. This was hardly likely to put him in a better mood. However strange his behaviour seemed, she was surely the cause of it and would pay the price. It wasn't long before his gaze was once more upon her. She opened her mouth to apologise but changed her mind. She didn't regret her words, only what would happen to her because of them.

'You're right of course,' he said, astounding her. 'I have placed you in an impossible situation and I apologise for it.'

'I don't understand.'

Never had she spoken more truly, and he astounded her further when his lips creased into a sardonic smile.

'I thought we had nothing in common, you and I, but I believe I've found something. We both say things in the heat of temper that we later wish unsaid. Would you agree?'

'Perhaps.'

'Then I will tell you two things I might threaten when you annoy me, but would never carry out.'

'Yes?'

'I'd never punish you as a scold. By the saints, Elinor, if you'd any knowledge of me at all you'd know that.'

Relief surged through her. She had his word. She mightn't know much about the man but she knew enough to know that a promise from him wasn't lightly given nor broken.

'And the other?'

'I'll never beat you. It's not in my nature.'

His voice was almost weary, and though she was grateful for his words she had to wonder at his tone.

'Thank you, William. I will try to be a good wife to you. I'll try to conduct myself in a way that never tests your resolve.'

Her words were sincere, so she was unprepared for the hastily concealed anger that flashed across his face. He shrugged, as though to rid himself of it further.

'No matter what you've done, no

matter what the law would say or demand, I promise I'll never do it.'

He stared at her as though awaiting a response, but all she could think of was to mutter her thanks yet again.

'Now tell me what you were about to say earlier.'

She hesitated.

'And if my answer doesn't please you, would you have me confined to the solar?'

He gave a great sigh of exasperation.

'Am I such a monster in your imagination?'

'You threatened me with it once before,' she whispered.

'So I did. How kind of you to remind me. And is this something else you'd have me swear not to do?'

'No, William, I'll trust you'd never do such a thing.'

She knew from the lightening of his features that she'd made the right response.

'Thank you. So tell me about the harvest.'

Elinor bit her lip. Was he always so persistent?

'Despite your absence, the people couldn't have worked harder. I thought it only fitting that they be rewarded.'

'In what way did you reward them?'

'With a feast, when everything was gathered in.'

'Is that not the common practice? Why should that displease me?'

She laced her fingers one between the other.

'Perhaps it was a feast more fitting for nobles than peasants.'

He began to laugh. It was such a merry sound after the discord between them that she could only stare at him. The harshness of his face disappeared showing her a completely different man, showing her the type of man he might be if they ever resolved their differences.

'I thought it might anger you,' she murmured.

He slanted her a look.

'And that is why you did it?'

'No!'

He waited.

'I wanted to reward the people for their hard work. I wanted to show them that their loyalty was appreciated, and . . . '

He wouldn't understand the third reason, and she wished heartily that she hadn't begun to tell it. She glanced at his face, at the stubborn, determined set of his jaw, and knew that she might as well tell him now. He'd have the answer from her eventually.

'And I did it because I'd never been able to before, because Gilbert and my father would never have allowed it.'

She waited with her head bent. Not only could he accuse her of being an undutiful sister and daughter but also an undutiful wife.

'Look at me, Elinor.' He smiled. 'I would much rather be known for the generosity of my table than for its meanness. Whatever your reasons, you did well.'

Her own smile reflected his, and she

realised that she'd begun to care what this man thought of her. Gilbert's opinion had never mattered and neither, in the end, had her father's. As a child, she'd tried desperately to make him love her but the most she'd ever managed had been his indifference. As she continued to gaze into the mysterious depths of her husband's eyes she was presented with a new lesson, the learning of which was a shock. For the first time she wished that he weren't so weak because she wanted to have him as a husband in deed as well as in name.

Why should she desire this? She knew that the consequences of the act could be dangerous, yet she looked at the strong arms resting on the bed cover and imagined herself locked within them. Flushing deeply as these unaccustomed thoughts caused a heated warmth to spread through her limbs, Elinor tore her eyes away from William's face and realised she'd been staring brazenly at him for some time. His smile had been replaced by a look of curiosity. By heaven, he might well be curious about what had passed through her mind, but in this instance he could question her until the day of judgement and she'd never admit it.

Had he read desire in her face or was it his imagination? A rapid pulse beat at her throat and her colour was high. He'd never seen her thus, and his own blood quickened. He brushed his meal aside and stood up.

'What?'

Her eyes widened as she became aware of his intention. She looked, he thought, like a doe surrounded by hounds. He must be careful not to hurt her. He must remember that she mightn't have done anything like this before. A small, startled cry escaped her throat as he reached for her.

'What are you doing?'

In order that she should be under no doubt, he encircled her waist and pulled her to him. Attar of roses drifted upwards from her gown and assaulted his senses. It was the scent that had always surrounded her. Even when he'd been unconscious the perfume had entered his dreams. Leaving one hand firmly about her waist, he lifted the other and removed her wimple. Her hair was beautiful. He smoothed his fingers over its soft lustre.

'Elinor.'

He bent to kiss her but was dismayed when she cried out. Only then did he hear the sound behind him.

Pushing his wife to safety, he turned to meet his assailant, and even as the blow struck he knew that he should never have been caught off guard. Spinning into blackness, he cursed his stupidity. He should never have had his back to the door. He should never have allowed desire to blind him to the possibility of danger.

Falling to the ground, he gazed into the eyes of his attacker until the darkness engulfed him. There could be no doubt in the matter — it was Elinor who had betrayed him.

Elinor clamped her hand over her mouth but it was too late. The guard had heard the commotion and rushed in. Gathering her wits, she dropped to her knees and felt for sign of life at her husband's throat. Merciful heavens! His pulse beat slow but strong. His skull must surely be fashioned from iron.

'Stand aside, my lady.'

The guard's voice was a deep growl and his sword was pointed at her. The blade gleamed long and sharp.

'I'm trying to help him.'

She failed to keep the fear from her voice.

'I think you've helped him quite enough.'

His gaze flickered over the remains of the shattered ewer before resting on Meg, who stood unnaturally calm and silent beside her. It must have been with the shock of what she'd done. To her knowledge, her maidservant had never felled a man with a jug before.

'You! Over there!'

The guard prodded her with his

sword, and the indignity of his action snapped her back to her senses.

'That I will not.' Meg folded her arms in defiance. 'Just who do you think you are ordering about, you uncouth brute?'

'Do as he says, Meg.'

Meg stared at her mistress without comprehension.

'That beggar was mauling you! Holy Mother, he'd snatched off your wimple and was going to . . . '

She aimed a kick at the senseless man below her.

'No!'

Elinor's cry was more a plea to the guard not to kill her servant than it was to Meg not to kick her husband. Thankfully the man had no taste for slaying women. He grabbed Meg's arm and spun her away roughly. She slammed into the wall of the chamber and slid breathless to the floor. Gesturing to Elinor that she should stand aside, he bent to satisfy himself that his master was alive before going over to Meg and searching her. The only item she possessed that could possibly be used as a weapon was her food dagger. Nevertheless, he ripped it from her belt before standing up.

'You can see what happened, why Meg should make a mistake. Sheath your sword, Thomas.'

His face registered surprise that she had remembered his name before growing impassive.

'All I know is that my lord has been attacked and that you were the only two in his chamber at the time. Begging my lady's pardon, but I'll remain until Lord William regains his senses and commands me otherwise.'

Elinor nodded stiffly before kneeling to comfort Meg who was bemoaning her harsh treatment.

'Oh, Meg.'

She shook as she took the older woman's hands and chafed them between her own. What would Meg's punishment be? And would she be able to prevent it? Her voice was little more than a whisper as she spoke.

'Thank you for trying to rescue me, Meg, but the man you thought to be mauling me had every right to do so. He is my husband, Lord William de Valences.'

As she came to understand the significance of what she'd done, Meg's breath came in short, struggling gasps.

'No,' she exclaimed, turning wide, frightened eyes to her mistress.

'It'll be all right, Meg,' she said with more confidence than she felt.

'It isn't him.' Meg shook her head almost off her shoulders.

'Look beyond the hair and the beard. It is him, I assure you.'

They both gazed in horror as the figure before them gave a sudden judder and lurched back into consciousness.

'Lord have mercy!' Meg clutched at Elinor's arm and began to wail.

'Quiet! Do you want to bring the whole garrison here?'

Elinor shook her until her moans

grew softer and mingled with those of the man before them who was struggling to sit up.

'So, I am not murdered.'

He touched his hand to his head and checked the fingertips for signs of blood.

'Nobody wants to murder you, William. It was a — '

He held up his hand to silence her.

'You are wrong, wife. There are indeed those who would murder me, but let us hear what your maidservant has to say on the matter.'

He turned his icy gaze on Meg. Meg's fingers dug into Elinor's arm.

'You're right, my lady, it is him,' she whimpered, then started to cry.

Elinor cradled her, whispering words of comfort in an effort to calm her.

'Hush, Meg,' she said as her cries grew louder. 'Tell my lord the truth and everything will be all right.'

The look of disbelief on her husband's face at this statement was not reassuring. He turned to the guard.

'Tell me what happened.'

'I didn't think to stop the old woman from entering, my lord. She's been in your chamber often enough.'

William nodded impatiently.

'After she hit me what did she do?'

'Nothing. When I came in she was standing like a statue. It was the Lady Elinor who was bending over you.'

'The Lady Elinor?'

William turned his gaze to her and despite her innocence she felt her cheeks flare.

'My lady wife? What was she doing exactly?'

'I'm not sure, my lord. She said she was trying to help you.'

Her husband's lips curved into a grim mockery of a smile.

'Ah. There are times when a man can well do without a woman's help. What think you, Thomas?'

'I'm sure you're right, my lord.'

William closed his eyes momentarily.

'Weapons? Were there any?' he demanded wearily.

'Only this one on the old woman.'

The guard showed him the food dagger.

'And the Lady Elinor?'

'I beg your pardon, my lord, I don't know.'

'It is well, Thomas.' He slanted a sardonic glance at her. 'If my wife had any weapons hidden about her person I believe I'd have noticed.'

Elinor maintained his gaze.

'Meg was only trying to protect my honour.'

'Your honour?'

'Yes, my honour. Recall if you will, my lord, what you were doing when my maidservant walked into your chamber.'

'Something so very distasteful to you?'

His face hardened into a black mask. Seeing it, Meg clutched at her arm and her cries intensified.

'Woman, will you be still? My head is ringing with your wails.'

'Can't you see that she's terrified? Please, William, she won't be quiet until she has your forgiveness for what she's done.'

'Or until she has a rope around her neck.'

'You cannot mean that,' she whispered, glancing anxiously at Meg, who had been shocked into silence though tears coursed down her cheeks.

'I've seen people hanged for less.'

'But not you, William. You wouldn't do such a thing yourself,' she said.

'And why wouldn't I?'

'Because loyalty is so important to you,' she said.

'Go on.'

'Meg was only doing for me what Thomas or Roger or any of your men would do for you. She thought that I needed help and, without thought to the consequences, she came to my aid. In a man, such an action would be deemed heroic.'

There was a splutter of amusement from the guard. William shot him a look and he fell silent.

'I'll not tolerate being attacked by

your servants, Elinor,' he said quietly.

'Of course not.'

'But you're right, I shan't hang her.'

'Thank you.'

'But she will be punished. You do understand that?'

'No.'

He stared at her a moment before shrugging his shoulders.

'It makes little difference, though I would have hoped for your understanding. But, with or without it, it will happen.'

'No, my lord,' she said, and was thankful that she'd had chance to utter the words before the look he gave her shrivelled them on her tongue.

'You'd better have good reason to gainsay me, wife.'

'Because it wouldn't be right. What happened to you was your own fault.'

There was a long silence, then a rustle of movement as William walked over to the chair in the corner of the chamber and sat down. A glance was all it took to see that he was struggling to control his temper. His gait was stiff, his hands were clenched, and a muscle pulsed in his jaw. Perhaps he'd distanced himself from her so that he wouldn't be tempted to strike her.

'Well? Speak, if you please. My patience is fast becoming tauter than an archer's bowstring.'

'I'm sorry for what happened to you, William,' she began, but her apology brought no softening of his manner. 'If I could have prevented it, I would, but I'd have had to disobey you to do so.'

His curse was mumbled but fluent.

'Elinor, my head is pounding. I'm in no mood for riddles!'

'It's no riddle. You told me, again and again, that I should tell no-one of your presence in this chamber, and I obeyed you. I didn't even tell my most loyal, my most trusted companion, who has served me faithfully every day since I was born, that the man she thought a stinking beggar was in fact her lord. I swear by all the saints that if she'd known this she would never have harmed your person in any way.'

His answer was a groan. He closed his eyes, rested his head back on the chair and said nothing more. Uncertain what this meant, she continued.

'You would be punishing Meg for the crime of loyalty. It wouldn't be just.'

'Enough!' His hand sliced through the air. 'My wits might have taken a pounding but I'm still capable of reason.'

'My lord?'

'Go, and take your serving woman with you!'

Elinor turned to Meg and felt a jolt of pure happiness as she saw the relief on the older woman's face.

'You've forgiven her?' she burst out.

'Forgiveness? You demand forgiveness as well? Isn't it enough that I forbear to punish someone who tried to crack open my skull?'

'I'm sorry, I didn't mean . . . ' The words died away as they encountered his stare.

'You may go, and take your serving

woman with you. You may return with some salve for my head and some fresh ale, but if she has any sense at all she won't climb the steps to this chamber again for fear that I'll change my mind.'

'Thank you, Lord William.'

Meg dropped to her knees. Afraid that her actions might annoy him further, Elinor pulled her roughly to her feet and bundled her out of the chamber.

Catching the guard's broad grin of amusement as he made to leave, William held up his hand.

'Stay a moment, Thomas.'

'My lord.'

'This tale will make a fine one to tell in the guard room, do you not agree?'

The man's lips twitched in amusement but he said nothing. William fixed him with a level stare.

'I regret that you shall not have the telling of it.'

'No, my lord?'

'No, Thomas. Not one word of what happened here will pass your lips. I'll have your word on't.'

'You have it, Lord William.'

'I value your friendship, Thomas. As a friend, I would like to ask you a question.'

The man nodded his agreement.

'What think you of my wife, Thomas?'

He knew it was unfair of him to ask it. They'd fought together as equals once, but his marriage had raised him to the position of master over this man.

'Speak freely. I'll not take offence,' he encouraged, as Thomas frowned in concentration.

'I think she's clever.'

William lifted his head in surprise. Of all the things he'd thought to hear, this wasn't one of them. A clever wife? He felt a stab of guilt as he recalled an unguarded moment when he'd been less than kind at her lack of learning.

'How so?' he asked.

'I'd have strung the old woman up if it'd been me, and I thought you were going to do it, but when the Lady Elinor had finished, there was no way on God's sweet earth you could lay a finger on the old crone.'

Despite the pain ringing in his skull, William's lips curved into a smile. He liked the idea of having a clever wife. What did it matter that she could neither read nor write? She was more than a match for him in any verbal combat. If only matters were that easy!

'By the bonds of friendship, Thomas, tell me truly, what do people whisper about my wife?'

Thomas scratched his head.

'Anything at all?' William prodded further.

'I don't like to say,' Thomas said finally.

'You have my promise that you'll receive no censure for your words. Indeed, you'll be doing me a service.

The man took a breath.

'They say that before the year turns, we'll be overrun with beggars that'll take the food from honest folks' mouths.'

'What? My apologies, Thomas,' he

added in a gentler tone. 'Explain if you please.'

'They say that it was never like this in the old lord's day. He'd have had them flogged if they'd come a begging, but that the Lady Elinor tells all and sundry to come to the castle gates for alms.'

William felt a stirring of anger. How dare people condemn his wife for her kindness?

'Just give the word, my lord, and I'll put a stop to it,' Thomas said, misinterpreting his master's change of expression.

William shot him a glance.

'And do my vassals go hungry? Isn't there enough food served in the great hall to fill their bellies?'

'Why, yes, my lord. I mean . . . er . . . '
He fell silent.

'Rest easy, Thomas. I promised not to take offence, and I don't.'

Curse his quick temper! The man would tell him nothing else for fear of sparking it again, and he was too proud to ask outright for the information he sought. At that moment, he heard a tread on the steps outside. At first, he thought it was Elinor but it was Roger Fitzhugh.

'What news?'

Roger withdrew a letter from beneath his tunic.

'The wine merchant brought it.'

'The king's seal?'

Frowning, William slid his dagger under the wax to lift it, and his frown deepened as he read the letter.

6

Elinor had been in the chamber some minutes before William registered her presence. 'The wine merchant hasn't yet left, I hope?' he inquired.

'He's with the steward.'

'Good. Send word that you wish to purchase everything he's brought.'

'Everything? But, William, some of his prices . . . '

'I believe we can afford them.' He gave her a strange look. 'Unless, that is, you've given away all our money to the poor at the gate.'

She flushed. 'I've always had a small amount of money for my own use. I know by rights that it now belongs to you.'

He waved her silent.

'Forgive me. It was ill said, especially as I owe my life to your charity. We need as much wine as we can purchase and anything else that we don't have in store. Henry is to pay us a visit.'

'The king? When? How many will he bring with him? Does the steward know?' She stared at him. 'Why should he come now when you're supposed to be with him at court?'

'Henry is God's anointed representative on earth and, as with the Almighty, one never quite knows what he'll do next. There may be a reason for him to visit but he hasn't seen fit to divulge it to me.'

'When do you expect him?'

'Two days.'

'Barely time to change the rushes on the floor and clean the tapestries. How many men?'

'The same as when we were wed.'

'The king will want to hunt?'

He nodded.

'So there'll be no lack of meat and we're well stocked with preserves. I'll call on the women from the village for extra help in the kitchen and for making bedding. I won't let you down, William.'

The look he gave her, like the man who gave it, was unreadable.

'In this matter, I don't expect you will.'

She realised that she was still clutching the pot of salve.

'Your head. Let me look at it.'

He shrugged away her fingers.

'It is well. Go to your duties.'

'It'll only take a moment. Let me see.'

She parted the thick black hair and probed until a groan indicated the spot where Meg had hit him. She pressed again to make sure. His answer was a muffled curse. She peered closer.

'Do you wear a helmet on the battlefield, William?'

He refrained from answering such a ridiculous question.

'You've no need of a helmet when your head is harder than any metal.'

She replaced the lid on the salve. 'And you've no need of this. The skin isn't broken.'

He touched his fingers to his scalp

and winced again.

'The skin mightn't be broken but there's a lump here the size of a hen's egg.'

He looked so aggrieved that she had a wicked desire to laugh.

'What a fuss you make, William. It's hardly the size of a sparrow's.'

'A sparrow's!'

He touched the offending spot again and his face darkened. She watched his change of temper with fascination. It reminded her of a wolfhound her father had owned that would allow itself to be stroked one moment and would bite her the next.

'I'm teasing you, William. Don't you like it?'

She'd wager he didn't, any more than she did. But there she was wrong. For a heartbeat he looked almost as astonished as when Meg had struck him, and then his mouth and eyes creased into a smile.

'You continually surprise me, Elinor.'

She stepped back and trod on a shard

of the broken ewer.

'I'll send someone to clear this. Will you throw off your disguise now that the king is to visit us?'

He shook his head.

'Not yet.'

'But you'll be with me when he does come?'

'You may count on it.'

That was a relief. She stared at him and wondered if ever the day would come when he would share his plans with her. He didn't intend to reveal himself as the master but he would be with her when King Henry came. It made no sense.

He smiled at her.

'You are beautiful, Elinor. Have I told you? If I haven't then I've been greatly remiss.'

She stared at her feet while her cheeks flamed.

'Don't mock me, William.'

'Mockery? There was no mockery intended. I find you beautiful, Elinor. I would have you know that.'

She heard the rustle of his clothes and felt the heat of his body as he drew close to her.

'Tonight,' he whispered. 'Tonight, Elinor, come to me.'

Her head shot up and glanced against his chin. So that was it! That was why she was beautiful all of a sudden.

'I'm your wife,' she hissed, 'yours to do with as you deem fit. You've no need of flattery to command me to your bed.'

He brought his fingertips to his mouth and touched blood.

'I find myself more in danger in the company of women than ever I did in the company of men.'

'I'm sorry.' She glared at him, her eyes denying it.

'Tonight, Elinor,' he growled. 'And not a drop of your foul potions or I swear you'll be sorry.'

* * *

She fully admitted she was terrified. In truth she couldn't have denied it for it was visible for all to see. The light from the torches on the walls flickered with a forbidding strangeness as she climbed the steps to William's chamber that night. He met her at the top of the steps and took her in his arms.

'Are you cold?'

'A little.'

'Then come inside. I bade Thomas bring an extra brazier.'

William seemed unaffected by the cold. Smiling, he stood before her clothed only in his shirt and breeches. Slowly, she lifted her hand and removed her hood. As she did so, her hair slid down her back in a cascade of auburn. Maidens wore their hair loose and, though this wasn't her wedding night, she came to him now as a maiden.

'Beautiful,' he breathed. 'But you are still trembling. Are you cold or are you afraid?'

'I am cold.'

'Come.'

He took her hand and led her to the bed, but instead of pushing her down on to it, he snatched away the cover and wrapped it around her shoulders. He then poured some wine and gestured that she should sit beside him on the bed.

'Taste this and tell me what you think of it.'

He handed her the cup.

'Strong.'

She felt it burning a trail into her stomach.

'Good. What else?'

He gestured that she should drink some more. She did as she was bid, then ran her tongue across her lips to savour the rich aftertaste.

'A friend of my father's brought some fruit back from the Crusade, round heavy things filled with red seeds. That's what this reminds me of, pomegranates.'

He reached out a fingertip to brush a drop of wine from the corner of her mouth.

'A good taste?'

She nodded her assent.

'Excellent. This was the costliest wine that the merchant had to offer but Henry should like it. It's only proper that we, as loyal subjects, check that it's suitable for the royal palate.'

'I'm glad that my husband takes his royal duties so seriously.'

He tilted his head in a mock bow. 'Drink some more. It'll warm you.'

It seemed to, or maybe it was the heat of his gaze that burned her as she did so. His eyes were like dark coals.

'Are you any warmer?'

She lifted the cover from her shoulders. 'I thank you, yes.'

'Let me see.'

He narrowed the space between them and pressed the palm of his hand against her cheek.

'Ah, yes, much warmer here.'

He trailed his fingertips down her neck and she shivered again.

'Not so warm there. And beneath your cloak?'

He slipped his hand around her waist and drew her to him.

'Mmm, quite warm. Let us see if we can do better.'

He brought his mouth to hers and her body stiffened.

'Don't be afraid of me, Elinor. I swear on my life that I wouldn't hurt you intentionally,' he murmured against her lips, and she relaxed into a kiss that was so soft and gentle she didn't want it to end.

'Stand up, sweetheart,' he commanded, and she obeyed.

'Not cold any longer?'

He turned her about to unloose her clothing.

'No,' she breathed.

'I'm glad.'

He crushed her to his chest, but as he did so she felt a sharp stab in the sole of her foot and cried out. He released her immediately.

'Did I hurt you?'

She shook her head and looked down at her foot but could see nothing.

'I forgot how small and slender you are. My apologies, sweetheart.'

'You didn't hurt me.'

He smiled at her and pulled back the bed sheets.

'And I won't hurt you now.'

And with that, he lifted her into his arms and on to the bed. Her foot throbbed. She must have trod on something hard, but what came next swept all thought of it away.

Afterwards, while he slept, she lay against his chest and listened dreamily to the steady rhythm of his heart. To think she'd been angered that he'd called her beautiful to coax her into the mood for lovemaking! Heavens, how easy it would be to be a good wife to William. From now on, she'd come willingly to his bed with no coaxing whatsoever!

She didn't want the night to end. She fought desperately to keep her eyes open, for it would happen only once in her lifetime that she fell in love with her husband. Never had she felt such closeness to any other person and she wanted to remember everything about it. But the more she fought, the more her eyes fluttered closed until all she could do was sigh in acceptance as sleep drifted over her. It wasn't as if everything would be changed on the morrow. This feeling of closeness couldn't be broken. It was too strong. They were united now by a power greater than both of them.

She woke to the movement of her husband climbing out of bed.

'Good morning, sweetheart. I didn't mean to wake you but I must go to the garderobe.'

On his way, he strode to the window, flung back the shutter and looked out.

'The castle still sleeps. You will stay in bed awhile yet?'

She smiled at him, admiring how the first watery rays of the day illuminated his body and accentuated its strong, manly lines. If her other duties had allowed it, she'd have stayed in his bed all day.

'Maybe a little longer,' she said as he left.

She stretched lazily and her foot caught the edge of the bedpost where it protested with a sharp pain. What could be wrong with it? She sat up in bed, crossed one knee over the other and brought the sole of her foot upwards to examine it. It had swollen during the night. She pressed the lump with her finger and felt something protrude. Carefully, using her fingernails, she managed to fasten on to it and pull it free.

As she did so, her foot started to bleed. Whatever had been in it had been acting like a stopper on a bottle. The room tilted as the sticky red substance oozed over her hands. She could stitch other people's wounds with a steady hand, but she couldn't bear the sight of her own blood. Fighting her feeling of sickness, she regained the presence of mind to press on the wound, and was bent over moaning softly when she heard William's voice.

'Elinor?'

She started, not having heard him return.

'What is it?'

'Oh, William, I've cut my foot.'

He recoiled as if she had hit him.

'Why would you do such a thing?'

'I didn't do it deliberately.'

'Did you really think to fool me with the trick? To make me see blood and so believe I was your first lover? Did guilt cause you to cut too deep?'

'What?'

He'd spoken the words but she couldn't believe that she'd heard him right. She watched in horror as he slammed his fist into the bedpost, and the noise reverberated through her very soul.

'William, I . . . '

The rest of the words died on her lips as she met the full force of his glare. He picked up his shirt and ripped off the hem.

'Would it amuse you to know that I counted myself the happiest man in the kingdom last night?'

He seized her foot and wrapped the linen around it.

'You're hurting me, William.'

'I thought you liked my treatment of you, wife. You certainly seemed to last night.'

She burst into tears.

'I did not cut myself deliberately,' she sobbed.

'Feet don't bleed for no reason, Elinor.'

He finished bandaging her foot, then pulled a sheet over her nakedness before reaching for his clothes.

'I trod on something last night,' she insisted.

'Don't play me for a fool, Elinor. I might have had my mind on other matters, but I think I would have noticed if the woman in my bed was bleeding like a stuck boar.'

'It wasn't bleeding then. It began to bleed when I pulled something out of it this morning.'

'Something?'

She looked about the bed.

'It frightened me so much that I dropped it but it must be here somewhere.'

His face was hard.

'I can't see anything.'

She swept her fingers over the coverlet. What could it have been?

'A piece of the ewer! That's what it was!'

There was a deep sigh.

'May I remind you that you sent a servant to clear it, and clear it she did. Since the dawn of time, no servant has ever taken so long to clean a chamber. I thought she was never going to leave.'

Elinor dug her fingernails into the palm of her hands. Why was he being like this? Why did he mistrust her so?

'Alice's sight is failing. It takes her a long time to accomplish the simplest of tasks. I'm not surprised she missed a piece.'

'Am I supposed to believe that you'd send a blind woman to my chamber?'

'She isn't blind!'

He shrugged.

'Not blind, but almost so, if you are to be believed. Pray give me one reason why you'd entrust so afflicted a servant with this task?'

'One reason? Are you sure that's enough? I can give you three.'

'One will suffice.'

'She needs to feel useful, William. She's worked hard all her life and needs to know that she still has a place here. And knowing that you want to keep your presence a secret from all but your own men, her dimness of sight seemed an advantage. And the other servants were fully employed making ready for the king's visit.'

'Then don't let me delay you here any longer. I'm sure you'd benefit greatly from an early start to your day.'

Though his voice was mild, she felt his rebuffal like a slap to her face. What more could she say to convince him? The wretches in her father's court had received fairer treatment.

'I was a virgin when I came to this marriage,' she stated.

How could he possibly think other-wise? She might have lived with her father's indifference most of her life, but on that matter he certainly wouldn't have remained indifferent. At best, he'd have incarcerated her in a nunnery. At worst, he'd have flung her over the cliffs to perish on the rocks below.

William didn't answer immediately. When he did, his voice was so low she had to strain to hear it.

'A virgin at our marriage? An interesting choice of words, Elinor. We were wed almost three months ago.'

Her cheeks flamed as she caught his meaning.

'I was a virgin when I came to your bed last night. I can say no more than the truth, and I've told you that already.'

She covered her face with her hands and wept.

'Tears can't change anything.'

No, they couldn't, but they would come anyway. She no longer had the will nor the strength to hold them back. When finally she wiped her eyes, he handed her her clothes.

'I bid you go now, Elinor.'

His expression was sad rather than angry, but she dressed as best she could without help while he turned his back and gazed out of the window. Perhaps he meant to show respect by it but, after the intimacy of the previous night, it was an insult.

'I'm ready.'

She reached for her cloak. It would hide the ties that hung loose at the back of her gown. He turned, came over and, with a face devoid of expression, fastened her into her clothes as deftly as he had unfastened them. He'd done this, she realised, many times before, and a stab of some strange new emotion pierced her heart. Last night had meant everything to her. To him, it seemed, it had meant nothing. Fresh tears seeped down her cheeks.

'William.'

She gazed up at him. Who was this stranger who was breaking her heart with his coldness? What had happened to the man who had made her his so gently last night? For a heartbeat, he returned. She forgot to breathe as he drew his thumbs in a half circle under her eyes to wipe away her tears. But then he pushed her away.

'Go now,' he said, breaking the spell that held them close.

'Shall I bring food to break your fast?'

'I'm not hungry. You may send the Alice woman after mass.'

She nodded miserably. So she was dismissed and he was giving her no reason to return.

'Elinor?'

Hope flickered as she turned back to him.

'Does your foot pain you?'

It did — a constant throbbing ache that seemed out of all proportion to its size. She couldn't begin to imagine what he had suffered with the wound that had almost killed him.

'A little,' she murmured.

'You'll be sure to bathe it and give it clean dressing?'

She nodded, though she was sorely tempted to let it fester. What was the point of keeping herself well? What was the point of anything when she had a husband who cared nothing for her?

7

He listened to her soft tread on the steps until he could hear it no more, and then he dropped into the chair and closed his eyes. A woman's tears! How had it come to this? How, after a lifetime of invincibility, had he allowed them to slip past his defences and lay siege to his heart? It had been all too easy. His wife had wept and all he'd wanted to do was gather her in his arms and swear that everything would be all right.

But he couldn't, not while suspicion hung between them to sully what had been the most perfect night of his life. Only now did he understand what the king had said to him two years ago at the feast of Candlemas. Henry had asked what frightened him most. Without hesitation, he'd answered that it was the moment in battle when both sides were awaiting the signal to attack. He managed to contain his fear until then but, to his mind, anyone who said they weren't afraid before a battle was a liar.

Henry, being Henry, had answered that he was never afraid, and William, being schooled in the art of the courtier as well as that of the warrior, replied that his comments concerned ordinary men and not the king, who had Divine protection. The king then confided that his greatest fear was facing his mistress's tears, and it was with the utmost effort that William had managed not to laugh in his face. His mistress's tears! And which one? Henry kept a larger stable of mistresses than he did of horses.

Now, for his sins, he knew exactly what Henry meant, and it was a hard lesson. Let a woman into your heart if you dared but know that you'd be defenceless for evermore against her tears. With a groan, he got up and began pacing the room. Had his wife cuckolded him?

Strange that he hadn't given it a thought last night. It had been perfect. For a short while he had known bliss, and if she hadn't panicked and falsified her loss of virginity he never would have doubted her. His fist crashed into the wall and blood welled on his knuckles.

How could she have been so stupid? For the first time in his life he'd found a woman who could have meant everything to him, whom he could have loved completely, and she'd destroyed it. He closed his eyes in pain and used every ounce of inner strength he possessed to block out thoughts of his wife. He was a soldier, not a poet. As such he should be using his brain to unravel the difficulties that the king's visit would cause him.

After a moment, he got up and called for the guard.

'My lord?'

'I'll ride today and meet with the king at Roxingham.'

'As Lord William?'

'No. I'll slip from the castle as a

beggar. You can form part of Lady Elinor's guard when she rides out this morning and bring me clothes, provisions, and most importantly of all, scissors.'

He flicked at his flowing locks with irritation.

'I can't tell you how much I'm looking forward to ridding myself of this, Roger.'

'Which horse should I bring?'

'None. It would be bound to draw suspicion. The wine merchant is waiting at Sareham with his stallion, an ill-tempered brute but one that should get me to Roxingham just after nightfall. Once off the estate, I'll don my hauberk and keep my helm down. I won't be wearing colours so I shouldn't be recognised.'

'Won't you take an escort?'

'A man riding alone is noticed less than a group.' He smiled grimly. 'Besides I'm trusting to the stallion to bite anyone who wishes to make mischief.'

'My lord . . . '

'You don't have to say it, old friend. Your face tells me plain that it isn't the best plan I've ever conceived, and if you can think of better then I'll be glad to hear it. I need to get out of the castle without being seen. I need to have parley with the king, and I need to ride back here on the morrow as Lord William de Valences, the bridegroom who left his bride and returned to court the day after they were wed.'

Roger gave him a look.

'It seemed the best of bargains at the time but I fancy if I could make it again I never would do it.'

Roger snorted.

'Then I'm pleased you won't have occasion to. I like you too much to countenance you dangling from the end of a scaffold. One doesn't deny the king, as well you know.'

Reluctantly, William had to agree.

'Aye, one doesn't deny the king, whatever the cost.'

'If that's all, my lord, I'll make preparations.'

'Not quite all. Ensure that you pick my wife's escort carefully today.'

'Of course.'

'And whatever you do, don't allow Robert Latimer to be part of it.'

The man raised his eyebrows.

'He rides out with her most mornings.'

'Not this morning. I don't trust him.'

'As you wish, but what reason shall I give?'

William pondered a moment but could think of none.

'Let my lady wife think of one. Women are cleverer at artifice. You may tell her that I only want my own men as part of her escort. You may tell her that I can't hold Latimer in the same high regard as she seems to.'

He saw by the expression on his friend's face that he'd said too much, and cursed his tongue. Whatever the state of his marriage, it was of private and not public concern.

* * *

'Well done, Martha. The king will certainly appreciate such fine stitching.'

Beaming with pleasure, Martha bent over her work with renewed eagerness. She might only be a lowly servant but at that moment Elinor envied her. She had three bonnie children and a husband who'd be proud to the end of his days of her sewing the sheets on which a king had slept.

With a heavy heart, Elinor made her way to chivvy the servants in the kitchen, but had scarcely left the bower when she encountered Robert Latimer making his way towards it.

'Robert, what brings you here?'

There was a harshness to her voice that was intended. She'd spoken to him before about coming here and wondered which of the girls she'd set to work in the chamber had caught his interest and caused him to disobey her. The bower was a woman's domain, and though he'd spent long hours here when they were younger it was no longer appropriate now she was married.

He gave an elaborate bow.

'My Lady Elinor, the sun has finally peeped over the horizon now that I am in your presence.'

She frowned. On cloudy days, he normally told her that the sun wouldn't come out for fear of being eclipsed by her beauty. If a man was bent on flattery, he should try to be consistent.

'I asked what brings you here, Robert.'

'Your ladyship.'

'Please state your business, Robert.'

She knew her manner was abrupt but she didn't have time for games. The king was coming and the castle was nowhere near ready to receive him. She mightn't have her husband's approval in the bedchamber, but she was determined to impress him with her domestic skills.

'My business, as always, is to serve your ladyship. To this end, I've been waiting in the stables in the hope of accompanying you on your ride, but alas have been waiting in vain.'

Elinor sighed. The last thing she could think about today was her own pleasure. Surely Robert should have understood that.

'I'm sorry, Robert. I should have sent word. I'm too busy preparing for King Henry's visit.'

'And your writing lesson?'

'The same.'

She so wanted to impress William with the progress she'd made, but it would have to wait. She continued to the kitchen, her mind calculating the vast quantities of food that would be necessary during the following days. Thank heavens she'd decided to over-winter more cattle this year instead of slaughtering them. If she'd followed her father's normal practice, there'd have been nowhere near enough milk for cooking.

'Lady Elinor!'

What now? She spun round to face

the tall, upright man hastening towards her, Roger Fitzhugh. She hadn't recognised the voice but she recognised the man, her husband's closest friend, the friend she'd incarcerated in the dungeon.

'My lady.'

He inclined his head in a bow and his mouth curved with humour. He knew that she couldn't look at him without embarrassment, and she supposed it was a small consolation for the harsh treatment he'd received at her hands.

'You wished to speak to me, Roger?'

'In private, if you please.' He guided her to the middle of the passageway that led to the kitchen. 'I have a message from your husband.'

Her heart beat faster. 'Pray tell me what he desires.'

'That Robert Latimer doesn't form part of your escort when you ride out this morning.'

'That's easily accomplished for I don't intend to go riding today.'

The man frowned. 'Lord William

wishes you to ride out.'

'Does he indeed? Then he can tell me so himself. You may tell him that if he wishes to speak to me, I am willing to come to his chamber.'

This was ridiculous. She wouldn't conduct her marriage through the intervention of strangers. The man gave her a strange look.

'He intends to leave the castle this morning.'

Her mouth dropped with shock.

'What? But King Henry's coming!'

He couldn't do this to her. She would happily have everything in order for the royal visit but he had to uphold his part of the bargain. He had to entertain the king.

'Pray let me pass. I'll speak to him.'

'I fear it'll be too late. I've been searching some time for your ladyship.'

Elinor bit back an oath.

'And when does he intend returning to his wife and estates?' she demanded.

Dearest heaven, how he demeaned her. That she should be forced to enquire of his movements from one of his men! Roger Fitzhugh's forehead etched into a deep frown.

'Why, with the king, of course. Forgive me, I thought you knew this.'

'With the king.' Her anger subsided. 'To maintain the pretence that he has been at court all this time?'

The man nodded.

'But he wants me to ride out this morning?'

'Yes, my lady, to give him clothes and provisions.'

'But why not Robert Latimer? I know he isn't one of my husband's men, but why name him in particular?'

'You'll have to ask Lord William that question, my lady.'

'And I've already told Robert of my intention not to ride. What shall I say to him now?'

The man lifted his head but said nothing.

'No doubt I shall think of something,' she said eventually.

She found Robert in the outer bailey,

lounging against the curtain wall and distracting the falconer from his duties. A flash of irritation swept over her. This was her fault. With everyone else in the castle working so hard, she shouldn't have allowed one person to be so idle, no matter that he was her childhood friend.

'Robert.'

She strode towards them and nodded curtly at the falconer who made himself busy at her approach.

'Of necessity, I must alter my plans and ride out this morning.'

Her mind had been wrestling with what excuse to give him, but in the end she decided to give him none. In William's absence, she was master here and no explanation was needed. She'd wanted to be so different from her brother and father, but it was churlish not to heed some of the examples they'd shown her. One such was that servants would obey any instruction provided it was given with total confidence.

He smiled and gave her an elaborate bow.

'I will accompany you to the stables, Lady Elinor.'

'No, I bid you go to the kitchen. You'll be serving King Henry tomorrow and will want to assure yourself that everything is in order.'

'But the steward . . . '

'The steward has other matters to attend to. I'm giving you this responsibility, Robert.'

'Responsibility is what I seek, my lady.'

'Good.'

That was easier than she expected. She turned away.

'I'm ready for the greatest of all responsibilities and have been for some time.'

'I can't promise, Robert. It's Lord William's decision.'

'Is he to return on the morrow?'

'That is my belief.'

'And you'll speak to him on my behalf?'

Her heart softened. Becoming a knight with land of his own was Robert's due. It was what he needed to give his life purpose.

'I'll try.'

'I am your servant for all eternity.'

'I'll be satisfied with the next few days if you ensure all runs smoothly during the king's mealtimes,' she replied with a smile.

★ ★ ★

Slipping unheeded through the castle gates, William felt compelled to turn and look back. As he did so, his teeth flashed white in a rare smile. Despite all his resolutions, his wife had filled his thoughts and there she was in the flesh. The smile faded somewhat when he saw who was standing beside her but, despite the foolhardiness of lingering, he continued to watch.

What a peacock the man Robert Latimer was with his bows and fine gestures! He'd met plenty of the breed at court and had often desired to place them on a battlefield to observe the fanciness of their footwork as they fled the action. He pulled the rag that served him as a cloak farther over his face as though for warmth and turned his attention to his wife. To his mind, she seemed more irritated than enamoured by Latimer's attentions.

She filled his senses as no-one had ever done and, by the same token, her deceit hurt so much more. Yet still the tiny flicker of hope burned deep within him. Could she possibly have been telling the truth? If she had, then he'd done her great disservice. He turned and hurried away. He'd need to make good speed to arrive at the meeting point.

Was she innocent? The question haunted his brain, and the farther he travelled from the castle the more he came to believe that he'd done her a terrible injustice. Cutting herself like that was incredibly foolish. He could have returned at any time and she must have known that.

Untutored she was in reading and writing, yes. Unpractised in the ways of the world? Possibly. But there was one matter in which his wife did not require teaching. There was one thing that she was not — she was no fool.

8

How handsome he was. Elinor had hardly stopped looking at her husband since he arrived with the king. Tall, close-shaven and arrogant, every inch the lord, every inch the king's man. What a difference fine clothes and cropped hair made to his appearance, but there was something else. Ever since his return, William's manner towards her had been that of a devoted husband.

At first she believed that he was acting a part, but the last hour had proved otherwise. He stroked her hair as they lay together and she snuggled happily against him.

'I don't think I've ever heard the king so generous with his praise.'

She smiled, remembering.

'He was being kind because of the place you hold in his affections. I'm sure the food and comforts here aren't any different to those he receives anywhere else.'

He kissed her on the brow.

'You're sweet to think so but you're wrong. The lavishness of our hospitality won't go unnoticed. You did us good service, Elinor.'

'I only did my duty.'

'The king thinks you're delightful.'

'The king thinks any woman who draws breath delightful.'

He gave a snort of amusement before tapping her lightly on the nose.

'Dangerous words, wife. I forbid you to repeat them to any but me.'

'As ever, my lord, you will find me a dutiful wife,' she said sweetly, and snuggled even closer.

'What a clever idea of yours to put Henry's coat of arms on the march-pane. He was most pleased.'

'Mmm, it was Robert's idea,' she said dreamily.

'Robert?'

'Latimer.'

She twisted away from him and sat up, remembering her promise. This might be the only chance she had to speak to her husband on the matter.

'He would have been a knight by now if my father had lived.'

She wondered if she should mention her suspicion that Robert was her half-brother but decided against it. If Robert himself didn't proclaim the fact then neither should she.

'Indeed?'

'I believe my father would have given him land of his own.'

'I see.'

She gazed at his face, trying to gauge his expression, but the candle had gone out and it was too dark.

'A knighting ceremony would be a pleasant amusement for the king, don't you think, William?'

'Hmph.'

'I would have asked sooner if you'd been here, but I'm sure it could be arranged in time. Robert could fast and spend the night in the chapel tomorrow and be knighted the next day.'

'No,' William exclaimed.

'Then when?'

'Never.'

'But my father gave his word that he'd knight him.'

'Your father might have given his word. I have not.'

'But he's lived in this household on that understanding.'

'Then perhaps it's time for him to seek his livelihood in another household.'

'But why?'

'Do you question my decision, wife?'

With a bound, he was out of bed and towering over her. She swallowed nervously.

'I wish merely to understand it.'

'Why? What is this man to you?'

'A friend.'

Why should her request have angered him so much?

'A friend?' His voice was nothing more than a growl. 'Then I advise you to choose your friends more carefully.'

'Why? What do you know about him that I don't?'

'I know everything, and I don't care to be played for a fool, Elinor. Knight him?' He swore volubly. 'The only time I'd lay a sword on his shoulder would be to hack it through his neck.'

He bent to retrieve the truckle bed and kicked it forcibly to the other end of the chamber then, without a word of good-night, he wrapped himself in his cloak and lay down on it. Deeply shocked, she stared at the stiff, unyielding form that was her husband.

'You're wrong, William,' she said. 'Whatever you are thinking, you're wrong.'

Later, as he lifted up the shutter that hung at the window, the first watery light of dawn fell across the bed. He'd stood here the morning after his wedding, watching his wife sleep. Would he never learn! He clicked his tongue in frustration and turned to gaze out of the window. There wasn't much to see — the stables and the castle dung heap.

How could she prefer this chamber to the other one? It made no sense, much like the woman curled on the bed behind him. He heard her snuffling gently in sleep, but far from irritating him, the sound evoked his protective-ness She sounded so innocent, like a child or some young animal that knows itself in danger.

Was she in danger? He pressed his forehead against the cold stone. She was playing a dangerous game, if game it was. Knight Robert Latimer! He'd sooner remove the man's innards and feed them to the swine. He moved around the darkened room unable to be still, and brushed against her gown hanging over the clothing pole. Attar of roses drifted upwards and, giving in to the weakness, he lifted it up and buried his face in its fragrant folds. Despite it all, he couldn't help still wanting her.

'You must get up now, Elinor.'

She was so lovely in sleep that he didn't think he'd ever tire of gazing at her, but he dared leave her no longer.

He'd heard the sound of footsteps hurrying towards the chamber and knew who it would be. She stumbled to her feet only half awake.

'Forgive me, William. I had no idea it was so late.'

She started to take off her nightgown, but he put out his hand to stop her at the same time as there was a quick rap at the door and it burst open.

'Lord William! You wanted to know the instant the king arose!'

It was his young page, who'd arrived with the royal retinue.

'Indeed I did, Alfred, but I could have waited the moment it took to answer your knock.'

'My lord?'

The boy gazed around the room and when he saw Elinor in her nightgown, blushed to the roots of his hair.

'I'm sorry, my lady.'

He bowed deeply, turned to go, and let out a yell as he hit his shin on the clothing chest. Half irritated, half amused, William shook his head as the door closed behind him.

'We've plenty of time. The king may be awake but will choose to breakfast in his chamber.'

His smile vanished as he turned to Elinor. Her face was aflame, and she held her gown before her like a shield. Filled with curiosity, he reached out his hand. Her flesh was soft and burning to the touch.

'We are man and wife, Elinor,' he said softly. 'There's no shame in it.'

'I know. Forgive me, William. It is so new to me.'

A feeling like the iron-shod hoof of a stallion kicked him in the gut. How could he have doubted her? This innocence couldn't be feigned.

'I regret if my actions have pained you, Elinor,' he said, and saw her light brown gaze search his face for meaning.

What she found there he couldn't tell, but he was glad she didn't ask him to explain. His rôle as a husband was one in which he was sorely lacking. For a man like himself, accustomed to excel in most things, he didn't like to dwell on it.

Once they were outside the bed-chamber, any shyness dissipated like morning mist. He watched, bemused, the manner in which she directed the servants to do her bidding. Within moments, trestles were being stacked against the wall of the great hall, the worst of the rushes taken up and replaced, and fresh white linen spread over the table on the dais. It reminded him of Henry rallying his troops before battle. Unlike the king, however, Elinor issued her commands in a quiet, measured tone, yet there was no mistaking her authority.

He followed her to the kitchen where she dispatched a boy to the village for an extra supply of bread in case the castle oven was unable to cope with the demands of their visitors. Her voice became harsher as she enquired why the three-day old bread hadn't yet been distributed to the needy at the gate, but softened as she bent to examine the burned hands of the spit boy.

'Lavender essence and clean bandages,' she directed, and a servant hurried away to bring them.

'My lord!'

A red-faced Alfred rushed into the kitchen and held on to one of the oak tables to draw breath.

'The king has left his chamber and is making his way to the great hall.'

'We'll be there directly.'

The page lowered his voice.

'He's not in the best of tempers, my lord. He's complaining that his head is beating like a drum and blaming the quality of your wine.'

William grimaced. 'Come. Let us bid our liege-lord good morning.'

His voice was resigned as he turned to his wife. She was chewing her lip as she sometimes did when lost in thought.

'Fetch me some willow bark as quick as you please,' she said to a serving girl.

'Elinor?'

'Draw me some fresh water from the

well and set a cupful to boil,' she said to another.

'Elinor!'

Now she looked at him.

'Tell the king that I'm sorry for his discomfort but will bring him a healing drink that will ease it.'

William pulled her to one side.

'I don't have much faith in your potions,' he hissed, thinking only of the one that ruined their wedding night.

'Such potions healed you,' she hissed back.

He hesitated. Perhaps she was right, but she didn't know the consequence if the one she prepared now made the king worse. In public, Henry was all smiles and friendship towards him, but in private he'd stated his disappointment at William's failure in his mission in the strongest of terms.

'Let the king heal himself,' he murmured.

It was the safest course of action. Henry's temper was unpredictable at the best of times.

'It will work. I know it.'

She laid a restraining hand on the sleeve of his tunic as he made to go.

'How can you be certain?'

'Because it worked on me the day after our wedding.'

His lips compressed into a tight line. Her gaze held his own.

'Trust me,' she beseeched and, to his own amazement, he gave way.

An hour later, Henry was congratulating him on his fortunate choice of wife and asking about the preparations for the hunt. It had almost ended in disaster. The royal taster of foodstuffs wasn't in the hall, and there was a heavy silence when Elinor offered the king her remedy. She appeared not to notice.

'I don't believe it's too hot, sire,' she announced, as though the only thing troubling Henry was burning his tongue, and she made great play of taking sips to ensure herself that the liquid was indeed the right temperature.

Nobody was fooled about her true purpose, Henry least of all, but after that he graciously swallowed every last drop and refrained from complaining of its bitterness. And she was right — it had worked. In this, as in other matters, he should never have doubted her. Today he'd glimpsed the woman she would grow to be, a confident, able helpmate who was easily his equal. This was the woman he wanted to share his life with.

And he'd allow no-one to spoil it!

He summoned Roger Fitzhugh.

'Bring Robert Latimer to me.'

9

Luckily, the hunt was a success and the tables groaned with the weight of the meat on them. During the feast she noticed that the steward was serving the king and wondered where Robert was. She asked in the kitchen, but nobody seemed to know.

The next morning, William pointed out of the window slit.

'I'd advise you to wear your warmest gown today.'

She looked out. Overnight the world had turned white with frost.

'Doesn't it look pretty?'

'Aye, you're right, though your friend Latimer won't share that opinion.'

The hostility as he spoke Robert's name was almost palpable.

'I almost feel sorry for the man. I well remember my own vigil. It was the longest night of my life, and though it was early summer the cold from the chapel floor froze my bones.'

'You intend to knight Robert today?' she said in amazement.

He nodded and turned away.

The mystery deepened as she stood in the icy chapel, buried her hands in the fur-trimmed sleeves of her gown and watched Robert's scowling countenance. Why on earth was he not happy? She turned to watch her husband who at least was acting as he should. His was a sacred duty, and no-one present would have guessed the animosity he felt towards the man kneeling at his feet.

There was a hush as William took the sword from the priest and held it aloft then the sword descended to Robert's shoulders and he was proclaimed a knight. Told to arise, Robert stood up.

She'd forgotten the accolade. William was now entitled to aim a blow at Robert. The blow was meant to be the last one that the new knight would suffer without being able to retaliate.

Though meant to be symbolic, she knew from her brother's laughing descriptions that some lords took full advantage of this free shot and delighted in punching their vassals to the ground. Poor Robert. His medium height and slight build were no match for the man before him. She clasped her fingers in sympathy.

She looked up to find William's gaze fixed on her, but looked pointedly away. He drew back his arm, curled his fingers into a powerful fist, and tapped the other man on the shoulder. Elinor stared at him, and this time when his gaze found hers his face creased into a grin. The ceremony was over, everyone hurried to leave the damp and coldness of the chapel.

Throughout the day, a question burned inside her, but it wasn't until they were finally alone that she plucked up courage to ask William.

'Why is Latimer not happy now he's a knight?'

William propped a pillow behind his

head and reclined on the bed.

'You were certainly generous in your gifts to him,' she added.

'Everything he could want for knighthood, including the land.'

'The land? I'd assumed he'd remain here as a hearth knight.'

'And the fact that he'll be leaving upsets you?'

'I rejoice in his good fortune,' she answered carefully.

'I've bestowed on him the manor of Saltcoombe.'

Now Robert's ill humour made every sense.

'The land is marshland, is it not?'

'But land nonetheless. Before my marriage to you, I was a landless knight for eleven years. I wouldn't have sneered at the offer of Saltcoombe. By the time I was born, what estates my father held had already been promised to my elder brothers. There was a time when I hated them for it. That passed, but the desire for land didn't.'

It was that desire that had brought

them together. She sighed. As each day passed, she was falling more and more in love with him, and when they retired at the end of the day, she felt that he cared for her. But perhaps it was his desire for sons that prompted his tender behaviour. His manner could change abruptly, and she felt sometimes that he still doubted her.

She climbed into bed. It would be better when the king had left. They would have more time to get to know each other. So the next morning, when the king announced he'd be leaving that day, she grinned at her husband, but he looked at the ground.

'I must leave with Henry,' he said quietly, and her world collapsed.

'You intend returning to court with him?'

'Yes.'

'You won't, will you? It'll be like the last time. I'll find you in a ditch, but you might not be so lucky this time. I might not be able to save you.'

He caught her in his arms and

hugged her silent. 'I'll be home before you have the chance to miss me.'

'I can't bear to think of you in danger, William.'

William thanked the saints that his wife had no idea of the danger she was in. Before he left, he'd made her promise not to leave the castle until his return. All his informants were united in the belief that de Riddington would take advantage of the coming festive season to launch his revolt. And he wouldn't think twice about snatching Elinor as hostage if the opportunity presented itself.

Several days later, William wrapped his cloak more tightly around his body and gazed out to sea. French ships would land at Erthwain harbour soon. He was certain of it. But what he couldn't be certain of was whether the men inside them would march straight to Winchester or attempt to seize the castles in their path.

Henry had laughed when he'd told him of his fears, and it had taken every ounce of persuasion he could muster to convince him to station a garrison at Sareham. If Elleston was attacked, reinforcements were but a day's march away.

And then he saw them. One sail, two. His heart plummeted as he counted ten and the danger to his wife increased. He dispatched a messenger with news of it to the king, then all he could do was wait for de Riddington's next move.

It came sooner than he could have imagined. The man had many faults but tardiness wasn't among them. The troops had barely drawn breath before they marched on Elleston. And for the first time in his life, William experienced true terror.

'The king's men will be here on the morrow, my lord.'

Roger Fitzhugh stood nearby. William came to a decision.

'As soon as it grows dark, I intend to return to the castle.'

'You'll be cut down before you put a

foot on the bridge.'

'I wasn't thinking of using the front entrance. I intend to slip into the moat and climb up the garderobe shaft. Fetch me some rope.'

10

There had been no loss of life. They'd been lucky, though the wounded lying on pallets in the great hall had begged for comfort before Elinor removed the arrows from their flesh!

Their stores were also dwindling fast. There couldn't have been a worse time for the castle to come under attack. Did William know of it? Would he be able to bring help before they starved or the castle was taken? It would be one or the other because she never would surrender to de Riddington.

With the fighting over for the day, she climbed the steps to her chamber with a weary tread. Her body yearned for sleep, but first she must tear what linen she could into strips for more bandages.

Her task over, she lay on the bed, but sleep refused to come. She lit another candle and as its light chased away the shadows, she resolved to write William a letter. If she didn't survive the siege, she could only hope that it would. As she toiled over the words, she heard strange noises and she gripped the dagger at her waist.

She bent to her task again, determined to finish so that she could sleep. There was a scraping sound that seemed to come from the garderobe. She ignored it. It was a trick of the darkness, nothing more. But the demon that suddenly burst into the chamber was certainly no trick of the darkness.

Brandishing her dagger, she let out a scream that would chase the very devil back to his domain, and it brought the guards. The demon held up its hands as a man-at-arms burst into the chamber.

'Sheath your sword, Fulke. It is I, William de Valences.'

Elinor tried to see underneath the filth to the man.

'At your service, my lady.' He grinned at her. 'And if it isn't inconvenient, may I trouble you for some hot water?'

As he bathed, she listened to how he'd sneaked into the castle. But she shook her head in bewilderment. As far as she could see, their situation was dire. All he'd succeeded in doing was imprisoning himself here with her.

'Why are you so happy?'

He took her hands in his.

'To see you alive and whole, sweetheart. I'd climb a thousand garderobe shafts to have it so.'

'And that was your sole purpose in returning?'

Her brain was having difficulty understanding his words though her heart was bursting with joy because of them.

'That and the challenge of eluding the French.'

'William, you could have been killed.'

'But I wasn't. Now, tell me what you were doing so industriously when I came into your chamber.'

He picked up the parchment.

'No!'

She'd written down the secrets of her

heart, because she thought she'd never see him again. He gave her a quizzical look, read but for a moment, and handed it back with a frown.

'You told me that you couldn't write,' he said quietly.

'Robert Latimer taught me.' She took a breath. 'After your reaction on our wedding day that I could neither read nor write, I desired that you should never again think me stupid.'

He swore under his breath before sitting down.

'When did this take place?' he demanded.

'Whenever I could find time. Before mass, after mass, before dinner.'

'Where?'

'At the table in the solar in the great hall. Where else? William?'

'I believe that I have done you great wrong, Elinor. I saw you and Latimer together. I saw him take your hand and I thought . . . ' His words trailed away.

'If Robert has ever taken my hand it's been to help me from my horse or guide me in my writing.'

'Can you forgive me?' His voice was little more than a whisper.

Her heart filled with even more love for him.

'On one condition. You must promise never to doubt me again.'

He rose to his feet and gathered her to him.

'I swear it with all my heart.'

'Then I forgive you.'

'It is more than I deserve. Now, come to bed, sweetheart. We must be up before first light tomorrow.'

Dawn was barely a promise when she awoke to find him dressed.

'I want to check the defences and speak to the men.'

'I'll come with you.'

Once she was dressed, he took her hand, and as they walked, he questioned her about the previous day's events.

'It all happened so quickly, William, and it was lucky that Robert returned when he did. Moments later and he'd have been cut off by the enemy.'

'Latimer? Latimer is in the castle?' he demanded.

'The road to Saltcoombe was impassable.'

'A lie. Follow me. It's best that you're not alone.'

He didn't stop until he reached the drawbridge and, while she dragged breath back into her lungs, gave instructions to the sentries on duty.

'If you chance to see Robert Latimer, I want him taken.'

'Why, William?'

'He has to be the traitor passing information to de Riddington. Stay with the guards! You'll be safe with them,' he shouted but she followed him.

When they reached the postern gate, he pulled her into the shadow of the wall. She heard the hiss as he withdrew his sword from its sheath and saw him frown as he gazed at the sentries guarding the gate. She couldn't blame him. Even from this distance, she could tell that they weren't awake.

174

'Stay,' he mouthed, and then, 'please.'

She nodded. She didn't intend disobeying him this time. Slowly, keeping to the shadows, he crept towards the gate. He reached out a hand to one of the guards and she saw the man topple to the ground. Then, even before she could cry out, an arm came around her waist and she felt the edge of a blade pressed to her neck.

'Robert?'

If William was right, it could only be him.

'Sir Robert, if you please,' he sneered.

'Let her go!' William yelled as he raced back towards them.

'Keep your distance, Valences, or she'll be dead before you get here.'

'Let her go, Latimer, and I give my word that I'll let you live.'

'Why, Robert?' she gasped.

'Because Elleston should have been mine! I was his son! Guy de Riddington knows it and will make me lord here.'

William's voice was calm and steady

in contrast to Robert's outburst.

'And so you fed him information, poisoned the guards and were about to let his men into the castle?'

'And will do so now unless you want me to cut your bride's throat!'

Elinor closed her eyes in terror. William might care for her but he wouldn't allow Elleston to fall into a traitor's hands. She heard him continuing to reason with Robert as he dragged her towards the gate.

'Why should de Riddington hand you the lordship of Elleston when he has three sons of his own and countless bastards besides? His promises disappear like snow in sunshine, as do the men he makes them to.'

Robert dragged her nearer the postern gate. If only she could struggle away from Robert for one moment, but the hand around her waist and the one at her throat held tight. She looked at her husband and saw his gaze drop to her belt. She'd forgotten the dagger that hung there! She grasped it and sank it in Robert's leg. Luckily, his reaction was to loose her rather than cut her. She was ready, and fled in an instant to be behind William.

He advanced towards Robert. The two men fought but the outcome was swift. Within moments, Robert lay on the ground.

'Come away, beloved.'

William wrapped his cloak around her and guided her from the sight.

'You're safe now. The king's men will be here shortly and my bargain to the king is fulfilled. I won't leave you again.'

'I do love you, William.'

'And I, you, sweetheart. You cannot guess how much. All my life, my only desire was for land and position, but when I saw you in danger I'd have given it all up to save you.'

3   8002   01285   8306

We do hope that you have enjoyed reading this large print book.

Did you know that all of our titles are available for purchase?

We publish a wide range of high quality large print books including:
Romances, Mysteries, Classics
General Fiction
Non Fiction and Westerns

Special interest titles available in large print are:
The Little Oxford Dictionary
Music Book, Song Book
Hymn Book, Service Book

Also available from us courtesy of Oxford University Press:
Young Readers' Dictionary
(large print edition)
Young Readers' Thesaurus
(large print edition)

For further information or a free brochure, please contact us at:
Ulverscroft Large Print Books Ltd.,
The Green, Bradgate Road, Anstey,
Leicester, LE7 7FU, England.
Tel: (00 44) **0116 236 4325**
Fax: (00 44) **0116 234 0205**